Heading up the road toward the house, Casey swiped an arm across her forehead and sighed. Then she sucked in air and caught a faint whiff of smoke.

Not cigarette smoke, but something heavier. She lifted her head and searched the darkness, barely able to make out the shape of the house. Fire? Probably just her imagination.

As she drew closer to the big plantation house, the sulphuric odor intensified. Suddenly an alarm went off, loud and blaring in the still night.

Fire! Bellefontaine was burning!

Her heart beat a drum roll of panic, and she began to run, her work boots clumping heavily along the dirt road. The yards separating the greenhouse and the house had never seemed longer. Her family was inside. Her niece, Megan, and Aunt Esme.

She burst around the corner, and her heart nearly stopped. Flames erupted from the kitchen window and even above the clamor of the alarm she heard Toodles, her aunt's miniature schnauzer, yapping madly. The dog never left Aunt Esme's side....

Dear Reader,

What red-blooded romance writer hasn't dreamed of writing about a riverboat gambler? I know I have, but since I don't write historical romance, I didn't think I ever would. Then Nick Devlin, the hero of *Casey's Gamble*, walked onto the page, and I had my chance.

So now that I had my hero, I had to think about a heroine who would suit him. At first glance, Casey Fontaine wouldn't seem to be the one. Along with her brother, Jackson, Casey is heir to the sugarcane plantation, Bellefontaine. Situated near Baton Rouge, Louisiana, the beautiful antebellum plantation is a sugarcane farmer's dream. It's certainly Casey's.

So how will Nick, a rover who's never had a home, fit with Casey, a woman with deep ties to her land? Come with me and see what happens as Casey risks her heart and convinces Nick to take the biggest gamble of all.

Casey's Gamble is the first book in the RAISING CANE trilogy. Next up is Roz Denny Fox's *The Secret Daughter*, and the final book of the trilogy is K.N. Casper's *Jackson's Girls*. Hope you enjoy all three.

I love to hear from readers. Write me at P.O. Box 131704, Tyler, TX 75713-1704. Or e-mail eve@evegaddy.com and visit my Web site at www.evegaddy.com.

Sincerely,

Eve Gaddy

Casey's Gamble
Eve Gaddy

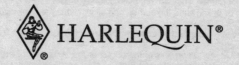

TORONTO • NEW YORK • LONDON
AMSTERDAM • PARIS • SYDNEY • HAMBURG
STOCKHOLM • ATHENS • TOKYO • MILAN • MADRID
PRAGUE • WARSAW • BUDAPEST • AUCKLAND

ISBN 0-373-71122-0

CASEY'S GAMBLE

Copyright © 2003 by Eve Gaddy.

This edition published by arrangement with Harlequin Books S.A.

Visit us at www.eHarlequin.com

Printed in U.S.A.

CAST OF CHARACTERS

Duke and Angelique Fontaine: Owners of Bellefontaine

Cassandra (Casey) Fontaine: Bellefontaine plantation manager and daughter of Duke and Angelique

Nick Devlin: Riverboat casino builder and owner

Jackson Fontaine: Bellefontaine business manager and son of Duke and Angelique

Esme Fontaine: Duke's opinionated sister

Megan Fontaine: Jackson's daughter

Roland Dewalt: Neighbor to the Fontaines

Murray Dewalt: Roland's son, and longtime friend of Casey and Jackson

Adam Ross: Nick's friend and historic home renovator

Vivian (Viv) Pontier-Renault: Casey's best friend

Luc Renault: Jazz musician and Viv's husband

Tanya Carson: Megan's nanny

Betty Rabaud: Fontaine family cook

Remy Boucherand: Police detective investigating suspicious events at Bellefontaine

DEDICATION/ACKNOWLEDGMENT

Although I was unable to go with my fellow trilogy writers on their research trip to Baton Rouge, I certainly benefited from it. I would like to thank Kenneth and Mary Jane Kahao, longtime sugar growers in the Baton Rouge area, for all the help they gave us in gaining information about sugarcane plantations as well as a working sugar mill.

If not for the generosity of Caroline Kennedy, director, and Jim Barnett, curatorial assistant of the West Baton Rouge Museum, our books would lack the history of the sugar industry.

Our apologies for any errors or bits of poetic license we may have taken in order to weave the fictional fabric of our linked stories. They are totally the authors' doing.

I also want to thank Captain Kenneth of the Hollywood Casino for answering my many questions about floating casinos.

Many thanks to Kathy Garbera, my wonderful critique partner. Much appreciation, too, to Lenora Nazworth for the information on flowers. And last, but certainly not least, many thanks to Christy Marchand for answering my endless questions about Baton Rouge, as well as for sacrificing herself to give me a bird's-eye view of Brew-Bacher's and their delicious shrimp po-boys.

PROLOGUE

"ANGELIQUE!" Duke Fontaine yelled up the curving spiral staircase. "If you're not down here in ten minutes, I swear I'll leave without you."

Casey Fontaine bit her lip and refrained from pointing out to her father that if he left without his wife the trip could hardly be called a second honeymoon.

Her brother Jackson came down the stairs carrying yet another piece of luggage, an expensive, flowered hanging bag. With a grimace, he set it down by the growing pile beside the front door.

Duke ran a hand over thick auburn hair, graying at the temples, and shook his head. "My God, how many clothes does one woman need on a trip?" He glanced up the stairs and his face softened. "But then, Angelique is always *magnifique*." He turned to his children and scowled. "Jackson, Casey, come into the study. I have some instructions for you."

"Let's see, how many sets of instructions does this make?" Casey muttered to Jackson.

"Fifteen and counting. But cheer up. Maman

can't have too much more to do. I think she's packed everything she owns. They'll be out of here soon. God willing."

"I'm really happy they're going on this trip around the world," Casey said. "But Duke's been driving me insane for the past two weeks. I'm not sure how much more of this I can stand."

"You and me both," her brother agreed, following her into their father's study.

It was a beautiful room, papered in a masculine brocade with gleaming wood and lush leather. A rich Aubusson carpet partially covered the hardwood floor. As always, Duke sat behind the imposing cherry-wood desk, an almost tangible aura of power emanating from him.

"You have all the numbers I left? And you'll call me if anything, *anything* at all comes up?"

"Of course, Duke," Casey said, laying a restraining hand on her brother's arm. It chafed both of them that their father treated them like children unable to think for themselves.

"Casey and I are perfectly capable of running the plantation," Jackson said, an edge to his voice.

Duke leveled a hard stare at him, then smiled. "You're wishing me straight to the devil, aren't you." When Jackson didn't answer, he laughed. "Don't worry, we'll be out of your hair soon enough. Assuming your mother ever finishes pack-

ing. Casey, go see what's keeping her. Maybe you can get her to hurry."

Her mother would be ready in her own sweet time, but Casey did as he asked, if only to escape the study and more instructions. When she reached the stairs she saw her niece Megan crouching beneath them. "Megan? Honey, is something wrong?"

Megan came out and looked at her solemnly, her dark, curly hair still tousled from sleep. "Aunt Casey, is Daddy—" She hesitated and dug her toe into the thick rug. "Is Daddy goin' away?" she finally whispered.

Casey squatted down to get on eye level. Poor kid. She'd only been living with Jackson for a few weeks, and was obviously still unsure about things. "Granmére and Granpére are going on a trip, honey. Not your Daddy. At least, not right now," she added conscientiously, remembering the business trips Jackson often had to take.

Megan sniffed and looked up at her, big brown eyes sparkling with tears. "Mommy went away."

"I know." Casey hugged her. "But your daddy won't. And if he does, he'll be back before you know it."

The little girl stared at her a moment, then nodded shyly. "'Kay," she said, and scampered away.

"Casey, where is your father?" Angélique asked as she glided down the stairs.

Casey glanced at her mother, wondering idly how the woman always managed to be such a picture of grace. Not much of that grace had rubbed off on her daughter, Casey thought with a grin. "In the study, Maman. He told me to find you and hurry you up."

Angelique smiled vaguely, her blond, perfectly coiffed hair glinting in the sunlight. "Dear Duke. He's always so impatient. I must have my makeup kit. My Louis Vuitton. You know the one I mean."

"But Maman, I thought you'd already packed your makeup." Oh brother, if she hadn't even packed that bag, no telling how long it would be before they left. Or how long it would be before some kind of peace settled over the big house. She curbed a sigh of exasperation, knowing it wouldn't faze Angelique.

"I do have a bag packed, but I discovered a rip in the lining and it simply won't do. I must have the Louis Vuitton."

"I'll see if Aunt Esme knows where it is," Casey said, resigning herself to a search through the attic.

Half an hour later, the entire household waved Duke and Angelique off. Casey looked at Jackson. "I guess a high-five is out of the question."

His lips twitched but he shook his head. "How long do you think it will be before Duke calls us?"

"Not as soon as he thinks." She grinned and shot a glance at her brother. "He told Maman to be sure

and take the mobile phone. I saw her dump it in the palm tree right before they left.''

Jackson laughed. "Good for Maman. Well, I'd better get to work.''

"That's right. We're in charge now, Jackson,'' she said.

"Temporarily, anyway. But that won't last a day past Duke's return.''

"Does it bother you so much?'' Casey asked. "That Duke thinks we can't run the plantation without him?''

Jackson shrugged. "Don't tell me it doesn't get to you sometimes, too.''

"Of course it does. Luckily for me, he's not as interested in the farm. And speaking of the farm, I hear the cane calling me.''

Finally, she could get back to doing what she really wanted. Growing sugarcane.

CHAPTER ONE

CASEY FONTAINE hated paperwork. Unfortunately, growing sugarcane in modern times demanded proficiency with a computer as well as traditional farming methods. She sighed and stared at the computer spreadsheet, filled with such data as type of fertilizer, yield ratios and the growth rate of the new hybrid compared to the growth rate of the other cane. It was often a boring part of her work, but someone had to do it.

When she left her office in the greenhouse where she'd spent the better part of the evening, her mind was fixed on the cold soft drink she planned on having the minute she reached the house.

The late August humidity lay thickly on the Louisiana air. The kind of atmosphere that slowed footsteps and made breathing a chore. Casey should have been used to it, since she'd lived on Bellefontaine, the antebellum sugarcane plantation near the Mississippi River, all her life, but sometimes the sultry weather hit her hard. This was definitely one of those nights.

Heading up the road toward the house, she swiped an arm across her sweaty brow and sighed. Then she sucked in air and caught a faint whiff of smoke. Not cigarette smoke, but something heavier. She lifted her head and searched the darkness, barely able to make out the shape of the house. Fire? Probably just her imagination, she thought.

As she drew nearer the big plantation house, the sulfuric odor intensified. Suddenly, a burst of orange and red flame shot from the rear of the house. An alarm went off, loud and blaring in the still night.

Bellefontaine was burning!

Her heart beat a drumroll of panic and she began to run, her work boots clumping heavily along the dirt road. The yards separating the greenhouse and the house had never seemed longer. Her family was inside. Her young niece, Megan, and Aunt Esme. Megan's nanny, Tanya. Everyone except Jackson was there.

But surely she'd have seen signs of the fire earlier if it was that intense. She'd have seen something— or heard something—when she'd first started walking home. The smoke alarm had only now gone off.

She burst around the corner, and her heart nearly stopped. Flames erupted from the kitchen window, and even above the clamor of the alarm she heard Toodles, her aunt's miniature schnauzer, yapping madly. Toodles, who never left Aunt Esme's side.

Shoving the back door open, she coughed and covered her mouth with her shirttail. Through the haze of thick smoke, she saw her aunt Esme. The older woman lay facedown on the brick floor near the old stove. The vintage one Esme insisted on using instead of the perfectly good modern one Casey's mother had had installed. Toodles stood beside her, alternately barking and licking the side of her face. For the first time in Casey's memory, the little dog looked happy to see her.

Quickly, Casey rolled Esme over, hooked her hands beneath her arms and started pulling her away from the fire. Her aunt was no lightweight and Casey's muscles strained with the effort. The slippery fabric of the robe her aunt wore didn't help, either. Toodles dodged in and out between her legs, nearly tripping her as she hauled her aunt toward the back door.

Flames shot out the window, smoke billowing up from the stove. The smoke was so heavy, Casey couldn't see how bad the fire was. Sweat dripped off her. She coughed, tried to wipe her eyes, then coughed more. She wanted to carry Esme, but she couldn't, so she dragged her instead. Finally, they reached the threshold, and as Casey glanced up she saw the fire leapfrogging across the room, coming straight at her. Desperately, she gave a last heave,

and she and Esme tumbled through the door to safety.

After pulling Esme farther from the danger, Casey collapsed beside her aunt. Coughing and retching, she reached to check Esme's pulse. It was strong, thank God. She hesitated, not wanting to leave Esme, but she couldn't afford to wait. She had to get Megan out. Bellefontaine was old, and for all Casey knew, the whole house could go up in flames any minute.

Esme coughed and mumbled, which Casey took as a good sign. She sprinted away, hoping her aunt would regain consciousness while she was inside. She ran toward the front, thinking that would be the quickest way to get to Megan. Gasping for air, Casey yanked open the front door and ran full-speed up the stately, curved staircase. The higher she climbed, the heavier the smoke became, until she was forced to cover her mouth again. The noise intensified, shrieking in her ears like a din from hell.

Oh my God. How can there be so much smoke? Already? Maybe the fire started someplace else. Her heart gave another lurch of fear at what that could mean.

The fire department! God, why hadn't she called them first thing? She yanked her cell phone out of her pocket just as she reached the top of the stairs.

Punching in 9-1-1, she dashed into Megan's room. *Hurry, hurry, hurry!*

"Nine-one-one," the operator said. "Please state your emergency."

Megan was sitting up in bed crying. Casey scooped her up, rubbing her cheek against the little girl's curly hair. She gulped in air and coughed before she could speak, then had to shout to be heard. "There's a fire! My house is on fire." Megan's thin little arms clutched around her neck.

The operator said something but Casey missed it. "The alarm's going off. I can't hear you."

"I show your address as 512 River Road. Is that correct?"

"Yes. That's right. Bellefontaine Plantation." She ran out of Megan's room and across the hall to Tanya's.

"We have the fire department on the way," the woman said calmly. "Are you in the house, ma'am?"

"Yes, I'm trying to get everyone outside." Flinging open the nanny's door, she yelled, "Get out! There's a fire!"

Tanya was sitting up in bed, her arms wrapped around her knees, apparently paralyzed with fear. At least, that was the reason Casey assumed the other woman hadn't responded to the alarm. The smoke

was so heavy Casey had a hard time seeing her, but at least Tanya hadn't passed out.

"What? What's that noise?" The young nanny coughed and glanced around wildly. "There's a fire?"

"Yes! In the kitchen. Hurry, I'm taking Megan out of here."

"Is the fire confined to the kitchen?" the operator asked.

"I don't know. I can't—I can't tell. There's smoke everywhere."

"Someone will be there soon," the woman said soothingly. "Can you stay on the line, ma'am?"

"No, I have to get my niece out. Hurry, please!" She stuffed the phone in her pocket as she, Tanya and Megan ran down the stairs.

They reached the ground floor and she thanked God again. Her chest heaved and she gulped in air, still smoky but not as thick as it had been upstairs. She ran out the front door and around the wide, curving drive, carrying Megan around back to where she'd left her aunt. By the time they got there, Esme was moaning and holding her head in her hands.

Casey propped Megan on one hip. The little girl was crying in earnest now. No wonder, Casey thought. She was probably frightened to death. She was only four years old, practically a baby. At least they were safe now.

"Are you all right?" she asked Esme. When her aunt didn't answer, she raised her voice. "Aunt Esme, are you hurt?"

Esme shook her head and moaned again. A moment later, she said shakily, "I'm all right. You see about *la jeune fille*."

The young girl, Casey thought. Even in a crisis Esme couldn't refer to her nephew's illegitimate daughter in a more familiar manner.

She glanced worriedly at the flames. They'd become worse in the few minutes it had taken her to get Megan and Tanya out of the house. Tanya came around the corner, pulling on her dressing gown, a silk confection that made Casey stare even in her preoccupation.

Megan was crying even harder now, so Casey sat down with her, rocking her a bit and trying to catch her own breath. "Hang on, sweetie. I'm calling your daddy." With shaking fingers, she speed-dialed Jackson's cell phone, praying he hadn't turned it off.

"Fontaine," he answered in his deep, familiar voice.

Relief cascaded through her. Whatever their differences, she could always depend on Jackson to be there when she needed him. Her words came out in a rush. "Jackson, get home right away. There's a fire at Bellefontaine. It's the big house."

"*Fire?* Megan?" His voice was sharp with fear. "Is Megan all right?"

Cursing herself for frightening him, she spoke hurriedly. "Megan's fine. We're all okay. Everyone's outside, but I have no idea how bad it is. I've called 9-1-1 and they said they're sending help. Hurry, Jackson."

"I'm close, I'll be there soon," he said, and the line went dead.

Casey glanced at the kitchen, fire blazing from the windows and door. She had to do something, she couldn't stand to just sit and watch while her home was destroyed.

"Megan," Casey said firmly, pushing the little girl's chin up so she could look into her eyes. "Aunt Casey has to go see what she can do to stop the fire. Will you stay here with Aunt Esme and Tanya? Your daddy's coming home as soon as he can."

Megan nodded and sniffed, her death grip around Casey's neck reluctantly loosening. She hadn't been living with Jackson for long, and while she knew and loved her daddy, she still seemed a bit unsure about the rest of the family. And no wonder. Esme for one hadn't been exactly thrilled when Jackson brought the little girl home with him. It gave Casey a pang that Megan seemed to trust her.

"Good girl," she said, and put the child in Tanya's lap. Casey gave her the phone, as well.

"Take care of Megan, and watch Aunt Esme while you're at it. And call Murray," she added, referring to their closest neighbor, Murray Dewalt. "I need help until the fire department arrives. The whole house will be lost if they don't get here soon." Tanya didn't respond other than coughing, but Casey saw she was at least hugging Megan. "Call Murray," she repeated, and gave her the number, though she wasn't too sure Tanya had listened to her.

Casey squatted beside her aunt. "Aunt Esme, will you be okay until the paramedics get here?" she asked anxiously.

Esme waved her away and pulled Toodles closer. "I'm fine, I said. It's just that my head hurts so." She rubbed the back of her head and frowned. "*Va-t-en!* Go see about Bellefontaine."

Casey dashed off to turn on the hose. It probably wouldn't make a dent in the fire, but it was all she could do by herself. Surely the fire department would get here soon. She knew it hadn't been long since she'd called, but it seemed like hours had passed.

She found the spigot nearest the kitchen and turned on the water, realizing when she did that the hose lay stretched across the lawn instead of coiled up neatly by the faucet. She pulled on the hose, only to come up short with a length of rubber sliced clean

through, about three feet away from the faucet. For a minute she just blinked, her brain too foggy to take it in. The hose had been cut?

Casey threw it down and ran around front to the other faucet. When she saw that hose stretched across the lawn, her heart sank. It had been cut, too, even closer to the source than the other one. Both hoses were totally useless.

Now what? She couldn't just stand around and twiddle her thumbs. *Extra hoses. The greenhouse,* she thought. There were more hoses there. She ran down the dirt road to the greenhouse. A few minutes later, she had a coil of hose draped over either shoulder as she ran back toward the blaze.

A large shape materialized in front of her. Casey tried to swerve, but so did he, and she ended up smashing into a chest that might have been made of bricks. Strong hands steadied her. "Damn it, Jackson," she gasped. "Get out of the way."

"Not Jackson," he said, his voice sounding amused. "Nick. Nick Devlin."

Of course it wasn't her brother. This man was a good bit taller. If she hadn't been so rattled she'd have realized that immediately. For a moment she simply panted and stared at him, barely able to make out his face since he stood with his back to the fire. "I don't care if you're the devil himself, as long as you're here to help."

He laughed and took the hoses from her. "Funny, that's what some people call me." The moon emerged from behind a cloud and bathed his face in light. Casey caught her breath, unsure whether the breathlessness was still from running or from the sight of a man she could only describe as drop-dead good-looking. Dark hair, chiseled cheekbones, a full, sensuous mouth that curved farther upward the longer she stared at him.

"You must be Casey." He didn't wait for an answer, but went on. "I'm a friend of your brother's. I was following him out here." He glanced at the fire. "Bad timing."

"We can use your help." She was really glad he was carrying the hoses. All of the running and hauling she'd been doing since she first saw the fire was beginning to tell on her. She was exhausted and having a hard time getting her breath.

"Don't you have hoses up at the house?" Devlin asked her.

"We did," she croaked, then coughed, her throat feeling like sandpaper. "But they've been cut."

"Cut? Deliberately?" he asked, his tone surprised.

"Yes, both of them."

"That's odd."

"Tell me about it. Where's Jackson?"

"Right here," Jackson said, catching up to them

as they neared the house. He took one of the hoses from Nick. "What in the hell happened to the hoses? Why are you dragging more up here?"

"Someone cut them." Her eyes and Jackson's met. "Deliberately."

"The hell you say."

"I know, it's crazy but that's what happened."

Jackson shook his head. "I don't understand, but we can talk later. Right now, let's hook these up and see if we can do some damage control."

Casey went with Nick Devlin to show him where to hook up the other hose. As he finished and turned on the water, a white pickup barreled up the drive and jerked to a stop.

"I'll be right back," she said to Nick, though she wasn't sure what more she could do with Nick and Jackson manning the only two hoses.

"Murray, thank God," she said, as two men climbed out of the truck. "I was afraid Tanya didn't call you." She wasn't surprised he'd come, just that he'd come so quickly. Murray was an old friend and a good neighbor, even if his father did have an ancient feud going with Casey's parents.

"Nobody called. Dad saw the smoke," he said, motioning to his father, Roland. "As we got closer, we heard the alarms." He took the hand she held out and grasped it warmly. "What in the hell happened here, Casey?"

"I don't know. I mean, there's a fire but the fire department is on the way, Jackson and his friend are using the hoses on it, but it's like spitting. I don't think it's helping any."

Murray took a considering look at the blaze coming from the rear of the house. "I suppose we could form a bucket brigade," he said doubtfully. "Using the water from the *garçonnière*," he added, pointing to one of the round lighthouse-type buildings flanking the main house. "But I'm not sure how much good that will do, either."

Casey shook her head. "Anything's better than nothing. Will you go get some buckets? There are some in the barn, I think. I'm going to help Jackson."

He nodded and went back to his truck. "Dad, I could use some help."

Roland, Murray's father, stood a short distance away, simply staring at the burning building. Casey suppressed a flash of anger. Why had he come over, if he wasn't going to help? Ghoulish curiosity?

"Don't worry." Murray put out a hand and squeezed her arm reassuringly. "I'm sure the fire department will be here soon."

A minute later, she found Jackson aiming the hose at the fire. Casey couldn't see that it was doing any good at all. She prayed harder for the fire department to show up, but Bellefontaine was some distance

from Baton Rouge, so it was no shock they hadn't arrived.

"Was Aunt Esme in the kitchen when the fire started?" Jackson asked her. "When I went to see Megan I tried to talk to her, but she wasn't making much sense."

"Yes, I found her on the floor. That's all I know. I don't know how it started, either."

A few minutes later, Casey left Jackson's side to check on Nick Devlin. Jackson wouldn't relinquish the hose to her, so she thought she'd try Devlin. "I can spell you," she said hopefully.

He shot her a glance and grinned. "Like hell you can. Go sit down. You're about to pass out."

"I have to help." She glared at him. It only irritated her more that he'd seen her weakness and called her on it. Fontaines didn't show weakness. "This is my home. Let me help." As soon as she said it, she winced. Her voice sounded forlorn rather than demanding.

He sized her up, then, apparently realizing her need to do something, handed her the hose. "Have at it, princess."

Another time she'd have taken exception to the nickname. But she was too tired and too scared to care right now. The only thing that mattered was saving Bellefontaine. She turned back to the fire with renewed resolve.

From a distance came the sound of sirens. She'd never been so happy to hear anything in her life. Smoke surrounded her, enveloping her in a dense cloud. Her eyelids felt heavy, her head began to spin, and the world went gray.

Casey opened her eyes slowly. She lay flat on her back in the grass. A man bent over her, dashing water in her face. A very handsome man, she thought, staring at him. She blinked and her mind cleared. Nick Devlin, that's who it was.

"What happened?" She struggled to sit up, but he pushed gently on her shoulder to hold her in place.

"Take it easy."

"I can't. The house, I have to help."

"No, you don't," he said, his voice surprisingly soothing. "The fire department is here. Let them handle it. They've got the equipment and the manpower."

"Thank God," she whispered, trying to ignore the tears stinging her eyes. She wanted to get up, but she was tired. So tired. She closed her eyes, then opened them again. "Why am I lying here? I don't remember..." Her voice trailed away. The last thing she remembered was praying for the fire department to show up.

She could hear them—the shrillness of the alarm, the men shouting, the water gushing from hoses, the

clang of equipment. The night took on a surreal quality. Was she really lying on the grass talking to a stranger while her house burned down?

"I brought you around front, away from the smoke. Your family's still out back, watching the firefighters."

The words rolled off his tongue in smooth, rich syllables, dark as night and twice as sinful. He had, without question, the deepest, sexiest voice she'd ever heard. From a man who wasn't a movie star, anyway.

His gaze intensified and he frowned. "But now they're here, you should have the paramedics check you out. Smoke inhalation's nothing to sneer about."

The voice might be sexy but the words did nothing but irritate. "I don't need any paramedics. I'm fine," she said, and immediately proved herself a liar by having a coughing fit. When it was over and she'd drunk some water, she sat up and gazed worriedly at the house. "What happened?" she repeated.

"Well, princess," he drawled, his smile a wicked flash in the dark. "You passed out in my arms."

CHAPTER TWO

"THEN, HOW FORTUNATE for me you were standing there, *cupcake*," Casey said.

Nick laughed, amused by the nickname. The "princess" comment had obviously gotten to her. "That's one I've never heard. In reference to me, anyway."

"Exactly," she said, her smile wintry this time. "I'm no more a princess than you are a cupcake. Remember it. Now that we've cleared that up, I'm going to see what's happening with the fire."

He stood and reached out to help her up. She eyed him a bit warily, but took his hand. He held on to hers a moment longer than necessary, though he suspected it would irritate her. Maybe that's why he did it.

So this was Casey Fontaine. Jackson had never talked much about his sister, probably with good reason. Nick's reputation with women wasn't exactly one that would make a Southern belle's mama dream of weddings. But then, Casey didn't strike

him as typical, not in any way, and sure as hell not with soot spread from head to toe.

She had the voice for it, though. Honey, with an overlay of smooth-sippin' whiskey. Hoarse from the smoke, she sounded like she'd just crawled out of a man's bed.

She pulled her hand from his grasp and strode briskly toward the back of the house. "How did you and Jackson get here so fast?" she asked when he fell into step with her.

"We were only a few minutes away when you called. We'd been down on the river, on the White Gold." He'd first met Jackson about seven years earlier, when he was managing another casino, that one on dry land. They'd kept in loose touch throughout the years, enough that Nick knew to look him up when the Baton Rouge opportunity came along.

Casey's brow furrowed and she gave him a puzzled look. "That new riverboat casino? I didn't think it was open yet."

"It's not, officially." And wouldn't be for another couple of weeks. He still had a lot to do before the grand opening.

"Oh. Do you have something to do with it, then?"

"You might say that." He'd had it built and had owned it, until a few weeks ago when he'd sold it to Guy Moreau. After he'd found a buyer, he'd

come down to Baton Rouge to oversee the initial
setup. Nick would hire the staff, and make certain
everything was running smoothly and that the new
owner could take over when all was ready. The
White Gold was Nick's fifth venture of the sort, and,
he'd decided, his last. Variety, that's what he liked.
He shot another glance at Casey Fontaine and
smiled. The spice of life.

She paid no more attention to him as they rounded
the corner and saw the chaos before them.

"Oh, my God," she said, and halted, staring at
the house. She covered her mouth, and he could almost feel the emotion vibrating from her.

Nick put a hand on her shoulder and squeezed.
"Steady. It's not as bad as it looks." He hoped. But
he told her what she needed to hear.

The sulfuric smell was strong, and smoke still sat-
urated the air. The wooden exterior of the kitchen,
as well as some of the rest of the house, was charred,
though there were no more flames. Several of the
men had climbed onto the kitchen's low roof. Nick
winced when he realized they'd punched holes in
the ceiling to get the water in.

"Look," he told Casey, pointing to some firefighters carrying a couple of large machines inside.
"That's a good sign. If they're taking those reverse
fans in to clean the air, then they must believe the
fire is out."

She gazed at him blankly, then repeated, "You think it's out?"

"Yes, otherwise they wouldn't be taking the machines in. See, they're shutting off the last hoses. But go ask the Fire Captain. He'll be able to tell you for certain."

She headed off, and Nick closed his eyes, unwillingly transported back to a scene too much like this one. Several years before, he'd been staying in an old hotel in Rothenburg, Germany, with a very beautiful *fraulein*. Someone had fallen asleep while smoking and the entire hotel had very nearly burned to the ground. Luckily Nick was a light sleeper and he'd gotten himself and the *fraulein* out safely. Others hadn't been so fortunate. He opened his eyes and shook off the memory. He'd survived. No point thinking about it now.

Casey had taken him at his word and cornered one of the Fire Captains. She'd apparently conquered her shock and was gesturing at the building while talking.

"Where were you and Casey?" Jackson asked, coming up to him. "I looked around and you were gone."

"Your sister passed out from the smoke, just before the trucks got here. Convince her to see the paramedics." He glanced at Casey, talking and waving her hands for emphasis. "I tried, but I don't

think she listened to me. She hasn't made a move in that direction, anyway.''

Jackson frowned. ''That doesn't surprise me. She is so damn stubborn.'' He sighed and added, pride in his voice, ''But I guess sometimes that's good. Casey pulled Aunt Esme out of the fire, and then went back in for Megan and the nanny.''

''Lucky for them she was around.'' So Casey was a heroine. It didn't surprise him, since she'd sure seemed like a take-charge kind of woman. Still, to single-handedly rescue three people and then take on the fire itself put Casey Fontaine in a class by herself.

''Very lucky. I should have realized she might be suffering from the effects of the smoke,'' Jackson said. ''Thanks for the tip. And for taking care of her.''

''No problem.'' Nick wondered what it would be like to have family who worried about you. Cared about you. It was something he'd never had, something he couldn't imagine ever having. But something he didn't miss. After all, you couldn't miss what you'd never had. But he found it intriguing.

A few minutes later, Jackson was literally dragging Casey by the arm over to the ambulance. Jackson was a few inches taller and his hair not nearly as dark a brown as his sister's, but there was a def-

inite family resemblance. Just now, the similarity lay mostly in their identical determined expressions.

As they passed Nick, Casey shot him a look of acute dislike. "Thanks a lot," she said, or rather, croaked.

He smiled as he watched them go. Casey was tall—five foot nine or ten, he'd guess—and slim, with dark hair escaping from a ponytail that flowed nearly to her butt. She was pretty now, even considering the effects of the fire. He bet when she cleaned up she'd be a knockout.

His stay at Bellefontaine might just be more interesting than he'd anticipated.

LATER, AFTER the Fire Captain in charge, Ted Mitchell, pronounced the house safe, the family gathered in the billiards room to talk to the officials. The family and Nick Devlin. Ordinarily, Casey didn't mind Jackson bringing his friends home. Especially not a gorgeous one like Nick. She was human, after all. But tonight was very personal, family business. And however delicious he might be, Nick Devlin wasn't family.

Thank goodness Murray and his father had gone home. Though Murray was a frequent and welcome visitor, relations were still strained between the elder Dewalt and the Fontaines. Neither Casey nor Jackson had ever heard the full story. Esme, usually ea-

ger to discuss all topics having to do with the family, wouldn't speak of the man at all.

Hoping to get Megan back to sleep, Tanya had taken the little girl to one of the *garçonnières* quite a bit earlier, after giving the Fire Captain her statement. Again, Casey wondered about the nanny's reaction to the fire. It didn't auger well for her care of Megan that she froze in a crisis. Casey intended to talk to Jackson later, though she wasn't sure yet what she'd say. She knew finding a nanny hadn't been easy.

Aunt Esme had flatly refused to let them sit in the front parlor or the living room, or indeed, any of the rooms that were part of the Historic Landmark tours. She had a point, Casey supposed, since they were all pretty grubby and could easily ruin the antique furniture and fabric in that part of the old house. What furniture hadn't been damaged by smoke, that is.

They couldn't be sure of the extent of the smoke damage yet, though the Fire Captain had assured them the department had run all the tests and the house was safe now. Casey had asked him a lot of questions before they'd all come inside.

"You won't even notice the smell upstairs after my crew gets through using the reverse fans," Mitchell had assured her, pointing at the open windows and billowing drapes.

She'd been doubtful, but he obviously knew what he was talking about. The room they were in now, though downstairs, didn't carry much odor of smoke, just a faint remnant of that and another stronger odor she couldn't identify.

Casey had taken a seat on the overstuffed dark-blue leather couch directly across from the huge billiards table dominating the room. Beside her, Aunt Esme sat in one of the matching armchairs. Both Jackson and Nick were at the octagonal poker table, in wooden chairs. They were waiting for the Fire Captain, who'd said he'd be there any moment.

"What is that god-awful smell?" Casey asked her aunt.

"Language, dear," Esme reminded her, frowning. "Ladies don't say 'god-awful.' Though I must say—" she wrinkled her nose fastidiously "—*c'est trés désagréable.*"

"Unpleasant? It smells like lemon crap," Casey said.

"Cassandra!"

"Well, it does," she repeated, unrepentant. Sometimes she thought Esme harped about her language—which wasn't really all that bad—as a matter of habit. Or possibly because she just enjoyed nagging.

"The smell is from a chemical called ozium," Nick said. "They spray it in the air, then use the

fans to clean the air of smoke. You couldn't stay in the house if they didn't use it.''

If he'd been handsome by moonlight, he was even more so in full, glaring light. His eyes were blue enough to drown in, a beautiful, mesmerizing blue as bright as the skies over Ireland, where his ancestors no doubt originated.

''You sound like you know something about fire fighting,'' Casey said, willing to be distracted while they waited.

''No, but I was in a hotel fire once. I asked a lot of questions.'' His lips twitched and he added, ''I like knowing about things.''

He didn't seem to mind taking charge, either, she thought, remembering how he'd hauled her away from the fire, then tattled to her brother that she'd been overcome by smoke. Though it had really bothered her at the time, she tried not to hold that against him. After all, he had helped them fight the fire before the trucks came. And he'd carried the hoses for her when she'd been about to collapse from exhaustion.

He was still looking at her, a half smile on his lips. Their eyes met, and whatever she'd been about to say completely deserted her mind. In fact, all rational thought pretty much evaporated. She found it hard to breathe.

Oh man, what's the matter with me? she won-

dered. All he'd done was smile and meet her eyes and she'd turned into a puddle of rampaging hormones. And a more inappropriate moment for these thoughts she couldn't imagine.

"Thank you all for meeting me in here," Ted Mitchell said, entering the room. He took one of the bar stools, piling his papers on the bar itself. "It's much easier to fill out the report with you all together like this."

Casey tore her gaze from Nick's and fixed it gratefully on the Fire Captain, who was holding his clipboard and scribbling on a piece of paper.

"I'd like to start with you, Miss Esme, if you don't mind. According to reports, your niece found you in the kitchen, unconscious."

"So I've heard. I'm not certain I was unconscious, though I was a bit stunned." Esme sniffed and regally inclined her head, clearly intent on putting her own spin to the events.

At sixty-one, Esme Fontaine was every inch the Southern society matron. Though she'd never been married, she carried an air of assurance that stretched back to her Creole ancestors on the paternal side, as well as the French aristocracy on her mother's side. Esme had been educated at the Sorbonne, and spoke flawless French as a matter of course.

Just now, she appeared more fragile than she nor-

mally did. It bothered Casey, because her aunt had always been such a rock. Esme's carefully colored, light auburn hair was a straggling mess, hanging in her face in a way that Casey knew would have horrified her aunt if she'd realized it. Aside from that, soot smudged both her face and her clothes. Casey doubted Esme had ever been so bedraggled in her life.

Esme wore a dressing gown of very expensive silk brocade, a gift Jackson had brought from Paris. Casey hoped it wasn't ruined, since she knew how much Esme loved it. Jackson was the apple of Esme's eye, or had been until he'd brought his illegitimate daughter home to live with them. Still, even that solecism hadn't caused him to fall below Casey in her aunt's esteem.

Casey didn't doubt her aunt loved her, but she knew she exasperated the older woman. Despite Esme's determined efforts, Casey had stubbornly resisted all attempts to have her take her rightful place in Baton Rouge society. Casey had neither the inclination nor the patience for the things Esme considered so vital to a woman of good family growing up in Louisiana.

Only when forced—usually by a gentle request from her mother, or worse, an abrupt command from her father—did Casey make a grudging appearance at the functions that were her aunt's raison d'être.

Casey just wanted to be left alone to grow her sugar-cane. Everything else took second place, or lower, in Casey's scheme of things.

"Can you tell us what happened, Miss Esme?" Mitchell had been acquainted with the family for some years now. He was also no dummy, and knew how to treat older Southern ladies. Politely request-ing information, with a touch of deference, drew her out infinitely better than barking questions would.

Esme nodded. "I came down to make some hot tea. I enjoy iced during the day, but there's nothing like a cup of hot tea at night, *n'est-ce pas?* The Earl Grey is my favorite. Do you like tea, Mr. Mitchell? My niece doesn't," she added, with a reproving glance at Casey.

Casey rolled her eyes but remained silent. An-other bone of contention was Casey's dislike of tea, iced or otherwise. Esme held firm that no true South-erner disliked iced tea.

The Fire Captain gently led Esme back to the point. "Yes, ma'am. Did you see any sign of the fire when you first entered the kitchen?"

"Well, I hardly know. Although I thought I smelled something a little odd, I didn't pay much attention. My television show was coming back on and I was in a hurry. Do you watch the Arts and Entertainment Channel, young man? Quite fascinat-ing. Tonight was a show about—" She caught her-

self. "But that's neither here nor there. I went in to put the kettle on to boil. That's when it happened." She paused dramatically, looking around at her audience to be sure they watched. Esme loved to be the center of attention.

"What happened, Miss Esme?"

"A man was in the kitchen. A great big ruffian of a man. I only caught a glimpse of him. I started to scream and he rushed at me. Something hit my head. The next thing I knew, I was out in the yard. Alone," she added, with another glance at Casey.

"What man?" Casey demanded. "Aunt Esme, you didn't mention this earlier."

"Of course I didn't. The important thing was to put the fire out."

"Can you describe this man?" Mitchell asked.

Esme shook her head regretfully. "No, I'm afraid not. I only saw him for a moment. Dark hair. And big and rough looking, as I said."

The Fire Captain from the other truck entered the room just then, going directly to Mitchell and conferring with him in a low voice. After a few moments, Mitchell nodded. "All right, you boys go on. I'll be along after I finish up this report."

He spoke to everyone else now. "Preliminary investigation establishes that the fire started with a pan of grease on the stove. There was a burner with a tea kettle on it beside the pan, but the burner beneath

the kettle was off. The one beneath the grease, however, was still on.''

Esme stared at him for a full thirty seconds. ''You're saying I turned on the wrong burner? Are you implying the fire was my fault, young man?'' she demanded imperiously. ''When I've told you about the man I surprised? Why, I never heard such slander in all my born days. You think I, a Fontaine born and bred, am lying about what took place?''

''No, ma'am. Not at all,'' the Fire Captain replied. ''I'm saying the fire was caused by the grease overheating.''

''There was no pan of grease on the stove I used. That woman,'' she said, referring to Betty Rabaud, their longtime cook and Esme's nemesis, ''wouldn't dream of using that stove. She'd better not, if she knows what's good for her. No, you're mistaken, young man.''

''Miss Esme, you misunderstand me. I think someone wanted the fire to appear accidental. This fire was anything but. Not only do we have your claim about a man in the house, and the cut hoses that Casey told us about, but I was just informed that the smoke alarm in the kitchen had been disabled.''

''So that's why I didn't hear anything when I was coming from the greenhouse—not until I was nearly there,'' Casey said. ''I couldn't understand why the

alarm hadn't gone off earlier, especially with so much smoke in the kitchen.''

Mitchell nodded. ''I think it's clear the fire was set deliberately.''

''I should say so,'' Esme said huffily.

Mitchell wrote some more down on the papers on his clipboard. When he looked up, he caught Casey's eye. ''Casey, I understand you pulled your aunt out of danger. Can you tell me what you saw? As exactly as you can describe it, please.''

Esme, still fuming and muttering about the perceived insult, distracted her. Casey took a breath and gathered her thoughts. ''I was walking up from the greenhouse when I smelled smoke, but I didn't think much of it until I got closer. I think the alarm went off just as I rounded the corner and saw the flames shooting from the kitchen. I heard Toodles barking and ran inside to find Aunt Esme lying on the floor.''

She closed her eyes, reliving the scene in her mind. The fear, the near panic. ''I knew I had to get her out. I didn't notice a lot, since I was concentrating on Aunt Esme, but the fire was getting worse, just in that short time.''

Mitchell nodded and took more notes. ''Did you notice a pan burning on the stove?''

''No. I didn't even think about looking for the source. I guess I should have pulled the pan off.

After I got Aunt Esme out, I was so worried about Megan, I went straight to get her.''

"You might have burned yourself severely if you'd attempted to move that pan, so it's just as well you didn't. What did you do next?''

"I ran upstairs and got Megan and her nanny. On the way up, I called 9-1-1. Why was the smoke so bad up there? I could hardly see.''

"Smoke rises. You shouldn't have gone upstairs, you might have been overcome by the smoke and fumes.'' He smiled at Casey to take the sting out of his words. "But with your niece upstairs, I can understand why you did.''

"Thank God she did.'' Jackson had begun pacing the room while the captain questioned Casey. "All this—'' he waved a hand, indicating the house "—from a grease fire?''

"You'd be surprised how quickly a house can go up. It could have been much worse. As it is, most of the fire damage is likely to be confined to the kitchen. You'll have possible smoke damage throughout the house, however.''

"You really think someone set the fire deliberately?'' Casey asked him. It seemed impossible.

Mitchell nodded. "Looks that way. We'll know more after the Fire Inspector comes out tomorrow.''

"But why would anyone want to burn down Bellefontaine?''

"I don't know, Casey. That's what the Fire Inspector will try to find out. Did anyone else see anything suspicious?" He glanced at Jackson and Nick.

Nick shook his head. "No, we got here not too long before the fire trucks arrived."

"We didn't see a thing." Jackson shook his head, as well.

Mitchell turned to Casey again. "Going back to Miss Esme's statement, you didn't see a strange man? Or any sign of one when you rescued your aunt?"

Esme bristled, but Casey ignored her. "No," she said slowly. "But I wasn't paying attention to anything except getting Aunt Esme out." Truthfully, she wondered about the existence of this mysterious stranger. Esme had been on the floor, overcome by smoke. She could have been confused. But then, the hoses had been cut, and the smoke alarm disabled. Those were facts. Very troubling facts.

"I know you think I imagined that man, but if that's so, then why do I have a lump on the back of my head?" Esme held herself rigidly. "Ask the paramedics—they treated me."

Jackson squatted beside her chair and patted her hand. "Aunt Esme, no one thinks you imagined it. We're just not sure of anything yet. We'll talk about it tomorrow." He turned to the Captain. "I think

my aunt needs to rest. Have you got enough for your report?''

Mitchell nodded and rose. ''Hank Jensen, the Fire Inspector, will be out tomorrow. Don't touch anything or try to clean up until you clear it with him.'' He hesitated a moment and added, ''I know it might not seem like it, but you folks are lucky that there's so little damage compared to what there might have been.''

Casey snorted. Lucky, yeah right. She hadn't the heart to look tonight, but the kitchen was probably destroyed.

After he left, Esme turned to Jackson and, in a voice that easily carried, said, ''Jackson, dear, you haven't introduced me to your friend.''

Jackson laughed. ''I guess I never did formally introduce you two. Aunt Esme, this is an old friend of mine, Nick Devlin. Nick, this is my aunt, Esme Fontaine. I brought him home to stay with us. He's, uh, working in Baton Rouge.''

''I'll leave you to see to his comfort. I'm really quite exhausted.''

''Do you want me to help you, Aunt Esme?'' Casey asked.

''No, dear. I'm quite capable of taking care of myself.''

Casey argued with her, but Esme was firm. She

left after bestowing a somewhat unfocused smile on Nick.

"Chicken," Casey said to Jackson after Esme left. It had suddenly dawned on her just what kind of work Nick Devlin was doing in Baton Rouge. She looked at Nick. "You're a gambler, aren't you? That new casino is yours."

"Guilty," he said, and smiled. "At least, it was mine before I sold it to Guy Moreau."

"Aunt Esme's going to kill you," she told her brother. "You know how she feels about the casinos." She turned to Nick and, in a passable imitation of her aunt, said, "Encouraging riffraff, and worse, to inhabit our city. But I'll let Jackson deal with that."

"No point telling her until we have to," Jackson said, seeming unconcerned. "Nick, I'm going to check on my daughter and then turn in. Casey, can you take him out to the other *garçonnière*? The one closest to the kitchen, since I put Tanya and Megan in the farthest one."

"But—" Before she could finish her protest, Jackson had tossed her the keys and left the room. Great, Nick Devlin, staying at Bellefontaine. She'd been sure her reaction to him had been a passing one, and since she'd assumed she wouldn't see him again, she hadn't been too worried. She had a feel-

ing ignoring him would be a lot harder with him under the same roof.

She looked at him and he smiled, a beautiful smile that made dimples wink provocatively in his cheeks. Her heart rate sped up. Hard to ignore? Try impossible.

CHAPTER THREE

"YOUR FACE IS REMARKABLY EASY to read," Nick said, enjoying the moment.

Casey got up and walked toward the French doors leading outside. "Is that a fact? Tell me, Nick, what am I thinking?"

"You're annoyed your brother invited me to stay. Especially now, with everything in an uproar. And you're having to be polite when you'd like nothing better than to tell me to take a flying leap. Am I close?"

Her lips curved into a reluctant smile. "Close but no cigar. And I do realize you had no way of knowing you were walking into a fire. Literally," she added, and grimaced. "It's hardly your fault."

"True, but don't let that bother you. If you want to take your mood out on me, have at it."

She choked off a laugh and opened the door. "Thanks, but I'll restrain myself."

He followed her outside, where he caught a whiff of river, even above the pungent smell of charred wood. "Can you see the river from the house?"

"From some of the upstairs windows. The levees weren't always this high, but then the Corps of Engineers started channeling the Mississippi so that it rises, rather than spreads out, the way it used to. That meant floods, so they built up the levees."

"You ever go down to the river and throw a line in?"

She stopped so suddenly that he bumped into her. At least he'd caught up with her now. The moon came out and he could see her staring at him as if he were crazy.

"Fish? Do I look like the sort of person who fishes?"

He considered her, then reached out and took one of her hands. The palm was rough, the grip strong, as he'd discovered earlier. "I don't know. You're nothing like I thought you'd be." Louisiana, old money, aristocratic roots—all of that added up to what he'd thought he'd find in Casey Fontaine. "I expected a decorative Southern belle who would be afraid to get her hands dirty. Obviously, that isn't you. You're not afraid of hard work. So why wouldn't you fish?"

"Fishing isn't hard work. At least, not the kind of fishing you're talking about. It's a leisure activity. I don't have time for it." She tugged her hand out of his and started toward the *garçonnière*.

"No leisure activities at all?"

"I don't have time for hobbies." They reached their destination a few moments later. She pulled out a key, unlocked it and shoved open the door. "The *garçonnière*'s pretty basic," she said. "Bedroom and bath upstairs, sitting room, kitchen and a half-bath down. In the old days, these were used as bachelor quarters."

He stepped inside and waited as she turned the light on and entered behind him. "So, what do you do that takes up all your time?"

She crossed to the tiny kitchen and started opening cabinets. "I'm a farmer. I raise sugarcane. That keeps me plenty busy."

He walked into the kitchen with her, watching appreciatively as she bent down to pull a coffeepot from the lower cabinet. "Too busy for anything else?"

Her head raised and her eyes narrowed. "Define 'anything else.'"

"Like I said, hobbies. Swimming, waterskiing, tennis." He smiled and added, "Gambling."

"Sorry, I get enough of the great outdoors from farming. And whenever I've gone to a casino and gambled, I've felt like someone was stealing my money. No offense," she added sweetly.

He chuckled at that. "None taken. So tell me about raising sugarcane."

"I can't imagine why you'd be interested."

"I haven't met a lot of farmers." Certainly not any as pretty as Casey Fontaine. "Indulge me."

"It's too late to go into the whole thing, but if you're really interested, ask me again another day. I'll tell you this, though. There's a lot more to it than most people think. We've been chosen by Louisiana State's bio-agricultural research center to test a new cane hybrid. That requires skill in raising the cane, and, unfortunately, a lot of paperwork." She glanced at him and her eyes flashed. "Farming isn't as simple as sticking something in the ground and watching it grow."

"I don't know much about farming, but I do know that."

"Sorry, I get a little defensive sometimes." She opened another cabinet and showed him the coffee and filters. "We usually have breakfast at seven, but obviously, that isn't going to happen in the morning. Unless Jackson goes into town and picks up beignets. You'll probably have to make do with coffee, here. There are some soft drinks in the refrigerator," she added, motioning to the mini-fridge.

Nick leaned against the wall and crossed his arms. "So, back to hobbies. What about men? Are you too busy for them, too?"

"Men?" She looked amused. "Men aren't a hobby."

"They are to some women," he said with feeling. "What do you consider them?"

She cocked her head and looked at him. "At the moment, a pain in the butt. Are you always this nosy?"

"Most of the time. It's a failing of mine."

She laughed. "At least you're honest."

Her eyes were a deep, jade green, crystal clear and beautiful, fringed with long, dark lashes. Bedroom eyes that sucked a man in deep and made him forget other women existed.

"I'm honest, all right. Can I tell you something?"

Her eyes took on a wary light. "That depends on what it is."

"Don't worry, it's nothing terrible. I'm very attracted to you."

She blinked at him. "What?"

"I said I am attracted to you."

She looked at him incredulously. "You're coming on to me? Now?"

"No, I'm being very careful *not* to come on to you." Though he wanted to. Badly. "I know, the timing stinks," he added.

"Yeah, you could say that. So let me get this straight," she said. "If we hadn't just had a fire at Bellefontaine, you're saying you would come on to me."

"Oh yeah. Definitely."

Casey stared at him, then laughed. "You're the strangest man."

"No, just honest."

"Why are you flirting with me, Nick?"

He smiled but answered candidly. "Because when I flirt with you, you don't look so sad and upset."

She grew more pensive, wrapping her arms around her waist as if to comfort herself.

Nick suddenly knew a completely alien urge to take that burden on himself. What kind of spell was she weaving? Why was he succumbing to it so easily? Women didn't normally affect him the way Casey did.

After a long pause, she spoke. "My home almost burned down."

"I know. It must be hard to take in." He'd seen how much it bothered her, and Jackson, too, when they'd feared the whole place would collapse. But Nick had never had a place to call home, had never been anywhere he couldn't leave as easily as he'd come to it. What would it be like to have a home, he wondered, one that had been in your family for generations? One that mattered to you.

"It is. I don't want to see the damage in the morning. I'm afraid of what we'll find."

"You'll feel better after you've slept. Maybe it won't be as bad as you think."

"Maybe." She walked out of the tiny kitchen and toward the door. Once there, she stopped and turned around. "So the flirting was purely altruistic?"

He crossed the room until he was standing in front of her. "Would you believe me if I said yes?"

She considered him. "No."

He allowed his voice to deepen, soften. "You'd be right. Smart woman."

"True," she said, and flashed him a smile. "Smart enough to recognize a flirt when I see one."

He watched her walk away and rubbed a hand over his chest. What a woman.

AS SHE'D SUSPECTED, Casey didn't sleep well. Her dreams were full of fire, smoke and fear. And if she wasn't dreaming about the fire, or lying awake worrying about how bad the damage would prove to be, she was thinking—or worse, dreaming—about Nick Devlin. He must be a devil, she thought, because she couldn't figure out why he'd made such an impression on her in such a short time.

Consequently, she didn't hear the alarm, and woke to Jackson banging on her door telling her the Fire Inspector was due in half an hour. Luckily, she'd showered the night before, but she wondered if her hair still smelled like smoke. She wasn't sure any amount of shampoo could fix that. She threw

on some clothes, an old T-shirt, jeans and sneakers, brushed her hair and ran downstairs.

At the foot of the stairs she hesitated, torn between putting off her first sight of the house in the daylight and getting the worst part over with. She squared her shoulders and went out the front.

It was as bad as she'd feared. The exterior was charred, parts of it badly burned. There were holes in the roof made by the firemen in order to get more water in. All the cabinetry had burned, and there were ashes where the table had once stood. She felt nauseated just looking at the wreckage.

After circling the building, she found Jackson on the back porch, a screened-in area that ran half the length of the house. Hanging ferns, potted flowers of all varieties, and heavy, plantation-style cane furniture made this area one of Casey's favorites.

Whenever she had some time, she liked to curl up with a book or magazine underneath the lazily turning ceiling fans and watch the wildlife along the levee. Or watch the birds clustered around one of the many beautiful fountains that graced the grounds of Bellefontaine. When Betty canned, the porch doubled as another kitchen. Luckily, it had a stove and refrigerator separate from those in the kitchen, so they would still have a place to cook.

Jackson was reading the paper, just as he did every morning. Except, this wasn't a typical morn-

ing. She nodded at him, then grabbed a cup and poured some coffee from the carafe on the table. "Where did you come up with the coffeepot? Don't tell me it was spared?"

He glanced up from the paper. "Nope. Raided the other *garçonnière*. I brought the microwave over, too. Megan and Tanya have already moved back to the big house."

"Good, the microwave will come in handy." Especially since that and a toaster were about the only cooking utensils Casey used. She took a sip of coffee and grimaced. "No need to ask who prepared this. It's awful."

"Don't gripe. You didn't have to make it," he reminded her.

"Have you seen the kitchen yet?" she asked, cradling her coffee cup.

He raised his head and looked at her. "I took a look first thing this morning. Unfortunately. What about you?"

Casey nodded. "Just now. Jackson, it's a total loss."

"Maybe. But I think it looks worse than it is. I'm sure we'll be able to have it restored, but it's going to take some work."

"I hope you're right," she said, and drank more coffee. She fidgeted a bit, then changed the subject. "Where's Betty?"

"Picking up some staples. And some beignets."
He shook out the paper and folded it.

Megan's favorite. Casey smiled, wondering what
magnitude of bribe Jackson had offered Betty to get
her to stop at the Dubonnet Café in town, a place
modeled after the Café du Monde in New Orleans.
Betty liked to make her own beignets, which, she
claimed with some justification, were infinitely superior. But Betty wouldn't be baking beignets anytime soon, not until things settled down.

"Betty will be here before long. With the kitchen
off-limits and smoke damaged to boot, we don't
even have milk or bread." He sipped his own coffee. "Tastes okay to me. But you're welcome to
make some more."

Casey threw him a dirty look. If anyone made
worse coffee than Jackson, it was her. Sometimes
she thought if Betty wasn't there to take care of
them, they'd starve to death. "Have you called Maman and Duke yet?" Casey couldn't remember a
time she hadn't called her father Duke. Some people
thought it odd, but the whole world called him
Duke…if not "The Duke."

"No. I checked their itinerary and they'll be unreachable for a few days. They're on a sailboat in
the middle of the Mediterranean Sea. I don't think
this is a conversation for ship-to-shore radio."

Casey winced. "You're right about that. It will

be bad enough over the telephone.'' Their parents' tour around the world was their first extended trip together in Casey's memory. Though Duke had left Casey and Jackson in charge of the plantation, he'd done it grudgingly. She knew he and Jackson had had words about it.

Casey and Duke didn't clash quite as much, probably because her interest lay almost completely in the growing of the cane, and Duke found farming the least fascinating part of the sugar business. But Jackson showed every sign of following in his father's footsteps. Wheeling and dealing came naturally to her brother. So far, Duke hadn't given him much credit, and even less control over the plantation or the business end of it. It had to chafe, though Jackson was usually good at hiding his feelings.

The Duke found giving up control difficult, if not impossible. It didn't matter to him that his son was twenty-eight, his daughter thirty-one. He didn't think they had the experience to handle things without him. It was only at Angelique's insistence that he'd gone on the trip at all.

''Actually, I think their being unreachable is probably a blessing,'' Casey said. ''Maybe we shouldn't tell them about the fire.''

''Not tell them?'' He looked surprised, as if the thought hadn't occurred to him. ''Why not?''

''It'll just worry them, and then Duke will be

chomping at the bit to come home. You know he won't think you and I can handle it.''

"True. And Maman has really been looking forward to this trip.'' He nodded and set the paper down. "It's not as if Duke's going to do anything we couldn't do. Except drag Maman home immediately once we give him the news.''

They looked at each other for a moment and then both smiled. "All right,'' Jackson said. "I'll tell Aunt Esme. I have a feeling she'll agree it's best not to tell them for now.'' He glanced out the window and called out to his friend. "Nick, we're on the porch.''

Nick opened the screen door and stepped inside, a coffee mug in his hand. Casey looked at it longingly. It was bound to be better than what she was drinking.

"'Morning.'' He nodded and smiled at Casey. "Didn't you say the Fire Inspector was coming?'' he asked Jackson.

"Yeah, he should be here any minute now.'' The front doorbell rang just then, a ponderous series of gongs.

Casey laughed as Nick's eyes widened. "One of the earlier Fontaines went in for gothic sound effects. Duke—our father—has always liked it.''

Jackson got up. "I'm sure that's Jensen. Are you coming, Casey?''

"I'll be there in a minute." Anything to put off seeing that wreckage again. Once had been bad enough. She fiddled with the coffee cups, pretending to tidy the tabletop. Seeing the destruction in the light of day had really shaken her. Even the Civil War hadn't brought Bellefontaine down. The thought of a grease fire doing what the Yankee Army hadn't been able to do made her cringe.

"Cheer up," Nick said, as if reading her mind. "It's not as bad as you're thinking."

He was far too perceptive for her tastes. How could he see through her so easily, when even her own family was fooled by her tough-girl facade? "No? Someone deliberately tried to burn down Bellefontaine. How much worse could it be?"

"They could have succeeded."

Her gaze dropped and she rubbed her temples. "You're right, of course. And no one was hurt. So it could be worse. But the house…the kitchen…"

"That isn't as bad as you're thinking, either. I took a look at it. The kitchen's probably a total loss, but at least from the outside, the fire doesn't seem to have spread any farther."

She made an impatient gesture. "I know, I saw it, too." There was so much work to be done. "We still have to find someone to restore it. Bellefontaine is a historical landmark. We can't just have any old

carpenter fix it. We need a licensed craftsman, and a person like that isn't so easy to find.''

''I can help you out there.''

Frankly skeptical, she said, ''Right. You just happen to know a licensed craftsman who specializes in historic landmarks.''

''Sure do. Adam Ross. He's an old friend of mine. Actually, he was one of my college roommates.''

''Is there anyone who isn't an old friend of yours?''

''You,'' he said, and smiled. ''But I was thinking you might be a new one. I'll get you Adam's number. Check out his references—I think you'll be impressed.''

Ross was worth a try. She didn't know of anyone, though Esme might. ''Thanks. If this works out, we'll owe you one.''

''Yeah?'' He gave her that devil's smile again. ''I like the sound of that.''

''Nick—''

He was suddenly standing a few inches in front of her. She found herself mesmerized by those incredible blue eyes. How did he do that?

''Have dinner with me.''

''What is this, more flirting in the line of duty?''

''Believe me, Casey,'' he said, his mouth lifting at the corners, ''I don't ask a woman out because I

think it's my duty. When I ask a woman out it's because I want to be with her.''

Unwillingly fascinated, she continued to stare at him. What would that mouth feel like if— She cut the thought off, irritated at her own weakness. Well, no wonder. She was grasping at any distraction, knowing she had to face the fire inspection. And Nick Devlin was some distraction.

Finally she said, "You move fast."

"Sometimes." He touched her hair. "Your hair is beautiful. But you know that, don't you?" He rubbed a strand between his fingers. "Soft. Like silk."

She stepped back and shoved her hands through the hair he'd been fondling, tossing it behind her. "It's just hair. I've been thinking about cutting it."

"Liar," he said softly.

Damn it, what was with her? She stuck her hands in her pockets and glared at him. It had been a long time since she'd met a man who actually interested her enough to consider going out with him. She wasn't entirely comfortable about that. Why Nick? Anyone that smooth was probably too much like her ex-fiancé, Jordan Whittaker. Suave, charming…and a notorious womanizer. She wouldn't make that mistake twice.

"Look, Nick, I don't—"

"Why don't you think about it?" he suggested.

It was on the tip of her tongue to refuse, but he brushed his thumb over her bottom lip, stopping her words. And nudging up her body heat by several degrees.

"Casey." Jackson opened the door and poked his head in as Nick's hand dropped away. "What the hell are you doing? Come on, the Fire Inspector wants to talk to you."

"I'll be right there."

Jackson closed the door and Casey started after him, grateful for the interruption.

"I'll be waiting for that answer," Nick said.

"It might not be the one you want." Wouldn't, if she had any sense.

Again, that dynamite smile lit up his face. "I take risks for a living, sweetheart."

She had no comeback for that. When she reached the door she turned around and looked at Nick. "I'll talk to you later." She shouldn't, though. What she ought to do was run the other way. Now. Any man who could make her forget her duty—forget the fire—even for a few minutes, was bound to be dangerous. The wise choice would be to turn him down.

Too bad she wasn't always wise.

CHAPTER FOUR

"GEE, THAT WAS FUN," Casey said some time later. The Fire Inspector had left, and she and Jackson had returned to the porch to discuss their next step. Esme, overcome by the destruction, had gone upstairs to compose herself. Casey was antsy, as she always was when the cane needed her attention and she couldn't get to it. They were gearing up for harvest, and Casey wanted to make sure everything would run smoothly. Instead, she was dealing with the fire's aftermath.

"Oh, yeah. I don't see how I can leave you with all this," Jackson said, pinching the bridge of his nose.

He looked tired—both physically and emotionally. The past few months had been a roller-coaster ride for Jackson. Although he hadn't married Megan's mother, Janis, he'd supported his child. He'd had visitation rights, as well, though Janis had made that difficult. The shock of discovering that Janis had been sentenced to prison for fraud and involve-

ment with drug dealing had sent him off instantly to bring Megan home to live with him.

"I'm going to cancel my flight."

Casey stared at him for a moment, unable to recall what he was talking about. "Your flight?"

Jackson nodded. "Remember, I was scheduled to go to Sugarland, Texas, tomorrow for the Sugar Coalition business conference? And then I was supposed to fly on to Mexico City next week for that conference on NAFTA."

"Oh, that's right. I'd forgotten." Jackson attended several business conferences a year. The one in Mexico City concerned the repercussions of NAFTA on the Sugar Coalition. "They're important, aren't they? The Mexico City conference especially."

He shrugged. "Doesn't matter. It's out of the question now."

"Don't be ridiculous, Jackson. I'm perfectly capable of handling things here. I do it all the time."

Jackson raised an eyebrow. "You don't deal with problems like this all the time. We're not talking about just the farm. We have to deal with insurance investigators, and at the same time, find someone to make the kitchen habitable again. And just between you and me—" he glanced toward the door, then back to her "—I don't know if Aunt Esme is up to it. She seemed awfully shaken earlier."

Betty, who was cooking bacon on the stove, snorted. "Better not let her hear you say that. Miss Froufrou thinks she has the last word on everything about this house." Betty often referred to Esme as Froufrou, the Cajun term for putting on frills. "You let someone she don't approve of touch that kitchen and all hell's gonna break loose."

Jackson shot her an irritated glance. "I'm aware of that, Betty. Leave Aunt Esme to me and Casey."

Betty huffed out an exasperated sigh, the unlit cigarette dangling from her mouth quivering in indignation. In all the years she'd known Betty, Casey had never seen the woman light one, but she was rarely without one either in her mouth or stuck behind her ear.

"Fine, but don't say I didn't warn you."

"We wouldn't dream of it," Casey said solemnly. To her brother, she said, "If those are your main concerns, forget it. I've handled insurance companies before. As for the repairs, Nick gave me the name of a man. It sounded like he was qualified. I'm going to check him out later today, and if everything looks good, I'll contact him. Adam Ross. Do you know him?"

He shook his head. "No." Jackson still seemed unsure, but after they argued some more, he finally allowed Casey to convince him it was in Belle-

fontaine's best interests for him to attend the conferences.

"But before you go, you have to tell Aunt Esme about Nick Devlin," Casey said. "You're not pawning that job off on me. He's your problem, not mine."

"You're making too much of it," Jackson said.

"Ha. Tell me that after you've told Aunt Esme."

"Speaking of Nick—" Jackson broke off and poured coffee into his mug. He didn't seem to know how to continue, glancing at her a bit too casually. "What was going on with you two when I came in earlier?"

Surprised, she replied, "I think that comes under the heading of None of Your Business."

"Look, Casey." He fiddled with his mug, looking uncomfortable. "I like Nick, but he's got a reputation with women that I'm fairly sure is well deserved."

"You mean besides being a gambler, he's a player."

Jackson nodded. "Well, yeah." He hesitated. "I'm not saying he's like Whittaker," he said, referring to her two-timing, disappearing ex-fiancé, "but he never stays long in one place. You should think about that before you go out with him."

She started to remind him that she was the elder sibling and didn't need him watching out for her,

but she knew it wouldn't do any good. He reminded her so much of Duke sometimes. Especially now, when he was in his "protecting the womenfolk" mode. What was it about Southern men?

"And don't try to tell me he didn't ask you out," Jackson added. "Because I wouldn't believe you. I'm just saying be careful."

"Thanks, but I'd already figured that out. Besides, Jackson, he asked me to dinner—not to marry him. Let me worry about Nick Devlin. You just take care of telling Aunt Esme."

"Tell me what?" Esme said from the doorway.

They both looked at her, then at each other. Casey raised her eyebrow. "Well, brother, dear?"

"Nothing, Aunt Esme," Jackson said hastily. "We'll talk about it later."

Nick opened the screen door and entered. He nodded at everyone, then handed Casey a slip of paper. "Adam Ross's phone number. I wanted to give it to you before I went down to the casino. I'm interviewing some bands for the grand opening today. Want to come listen?"

Casey nearly groaned. Talk about bad timing. "Thanks," she said, taking the paper. "And thanks for the invite, but I have too much to do here."

"I was afraid you would, but I thought I'd ask."

"Casino?" Esme echoed sharply. "What's this about a casino?"

"The White Gold," Nick said. "The newest riverboat casino. I'm getting it ready for the grand opening. It's set for a week from Friday."

Esme stared at him for a full minute, looking him up and down in revulsion. "Jackson." She turned to her nephew, wrath kindling in her eyes. "You brought a casino owner into our home? Without even telling me?"

"Oh, I'm no longer the owner," Nick said, before Jackson could answer. "I sold it. I'm just managing it until it's up and running." He winked at Casey.

Much as she wanted to, Casey couldn't find the humor in the situation. Esme was at her intolerant worst, Jackson looked like a thundercloud about to burst, and she was so irritated she wanted to scream. She took Nick's arm and tried to hustle him out before the storm broke.

"Thanks so much. Don't let us keep you," she said.

"You know my feelings about those casinos, Jackson. Dens of iniquity, that's what they are. Encouraging the criminal elements to inhabit our city. How could you? I forbid it, do you hear me? He can't stay here."

"The hell he can't," Jackson said, his temper rising to meet hers. "I'll invite anyone I please to my own home."

"Of course you will. You've shown no consid-

eration for the rest of your family,'' Esme said.
''First it's your il   '' she bit her lip ''—your daughter, now it's riverboat gamblers. What will be next,
a woman of ill repute?''

Betty had turned around and crossed her arms,
preparing to enjoy the fireworks. Casey wanted to
sink into the floor.

''Come on,'' Casey said to Nick. ''Let's get out
of here.''

He grinned down at her. ''Don't worry, I'm no-
toriously thick-skinned.''

''Yes, but I'm not.'' He might not mind, but she
was mortified. ''Come on, Jackson can deal with
her. Serves him right,'' she muttered. She practically
dragged him to the door and shoved him out. ''See
you later,'' she threw over her shoulder, but the bat-
tle raged, the dog barked, and neither her brother
nor her aunt heard her.

''Stop laughing,'' Casey said crossly, as they
walked down the back drive toward a car—a sweet
little red Porsche, unless she missed her guess—
parked some distance away. The man had good
taste. In cars, anyway. ''There's nothing funny about
it.''

He stopped and pushed her chin up with his fingers, gazing into her eyes. She looked back at him
defiantly as his own gaze softened.

"Hey, there's nothing to be embarrassed about. I've had much worse said to me, believe me."

Casey jerked away, conscious of a warm feeling in the pit of her stomach. She knew what it was. Pleasure at his touch. *Entirely too dangerous.* She shrugged off her conflicting emotions and mentally straightened her back.

"Jackson should have told her before now. Aunt Esme has some kind of grudge against the casinos, especially the boats. It's nothing against you personally. But it would be best if you just avoided her for a few days, at least."

"Not a problem. As long as I don't have to avoid you." The color of his eyes deepened, and he stroked a finger along the side of her face. A shiver went down her spine, even as she lectured herself. No way was she falling for another fly-by-night man. She took a step back, remembering Jackson's warning. Not that she'd needed it.

No doubt Nick Devlin knew everything there was to know about getting past a woman's defenses. Not to mention, into her pants. She wished that thought angered her, rather than intrigued her. "You don't have to avoid me. But I'm not going out with you."

"Why not?"

She decided to tell him the truth. Casey believed in being up-front with people. Especially men, es-

pecially after the fiasco with her ex-fiancé. "You're a very attractive man."

One corner of his mouth lifted. "Thanks. Do I hear a 'but' after that?"

She nodded. "But I'm not in the market for a summer fling. So there's really no point in our seeing each other. It's not going to lead anywhere."

"You mean, it's not going to lead to us sleeping together."

"Right."

He looked amused, which annoyed her. "Tell me something, Casey. Have you ever *had* a summer fling?"

"Of course I—" She broke off. Truthfully, she hadn't. Every relationship she'd had—all three of them—had been long term. Committed. Or at least, on her part they'd been committed.

"What does that have to do with anything?"

"Not a thing, sweetheart." He opened the car door and slid in, then rolled down the window. "But I'd suggest you don't knock it until you've tried it."

Casey leaned down to the open window. "*You* tell *me* something. Have you ever tried sticking around?"

He looked thoughtful, then flashed her a grin. "Can't say that I have. But there's a reason for that—"

Casey merely lifted an eyebrow and waited.

"I've never met a woman I thought was worth sticking around for." He put the car in gear, and she took a step back. "Yet," he added, in that deep, sexy voice, and then drove off.

He was smart, all right. What self-respecting woman could resist such a challenge?

Me, she told herself. *I will not buy into this game. Nope, no way. "Don't knock it until you've tried it,"* he'd said.

"Ha," she muttered, and turned toward the fields. "I haven't tried hara-kiri, either. That doesn't mean I'm going to run right out and buy a sword, just so I can say I've done it."

THREE DAYS LATER Nick sat on the White Gold, interviewing musicians for what he devoutly hoped was the last time. He'd heard some good ones, even some he'd hired to play at the grand opening and at later dates. But he hadn't found "the" musician. The headliner for the grand opening.

Besides gambling, the White Gold would offer fine dining and entertainment. He wanted someone special to open, someone unique. They didn't have to be well-known. He wouldn't mind a sleeper who had the potential to explode. In fact, he decided, he'd prefer it.

The top floor of the boat was given over to an exclusive gaming room for the high rollers, com-

plete with baccarat, blackjack, roulette and poker—
all at a very stiff minimum. Next to this was a posh
dining room and bar for those who'd had enough of
gambling for the moment. One end of the dining
room held a raised stage for various comedy acts or
bands, as well as a parquet dance floor.

Nick looked around the large room, satisfied with
what he saw. He'd hired two maître d's yesterday
who came highly recommended. The furnishings reminded him of the riverboat scene from *Gone With
the Wind,* which had been his intention when he'd
hired the interior designer.

Lush red velvet hangings, snowy white tablecloths and a gleaming, polished dark wood mahogany bar that ran half the length of one wall. Classy,
quiet elegance, a direct contrast to the more raucous
rooms on the floors below. The White Gold would
have something for everyone, from the serious gambler to the curious who just wanted to drop a few
bucks in a nickel slot and watch the action.

Yesterday he'd signed the deal with the fourth
captain. Though casino boats didn't take to the water
after their initial move downriver from St. Louis, the
Coast Guard still required them to have a fully licensed captain on board at all times. The boat would
undergo regular Coast Guard inspections, just as
every maritime vessel must do. Nick didn't question
why, he merely complied with the law. But he did

occasionally wonder why a vessel that would never be fully seaworthy had to pass such stringent inspection—beyond fire codes, of course.

He picked up his club soda and sipped it. Maybe the problem wasn't lack of talent. Maybe he was the problem. He hadn't seen Casey except at a distance in three days. Who'd have thought one woman would have him so intrigued he couldn't even consider other women? Just last night he'd turned down an invitation from a very attractive female jazz singer, and it hadn't caused him a pang of regret.

He'd given Casey enough time. He intended to find out tonight if she'd meant what she said about not going out with him, or if she regretted those hasty words.

The next band, a jazz band headed by an alto sax player named Luc Renault, had finished setting up. Nick watched with a grin as a very classy blonde wrapped her arms around Luc and laid a kiss on him that should have steamed the paint off the walls. "Break a leg," he heard her say before she took a seat at a front-row table. Nick doubted he was the only man who watched her go.

The sax player took it in stride, though. "*Merci, bébé,*" he told her, and launched into their first number.

Nick knew he had his headliner after the first riff. By the time the band had gone to their second song,

he simply listened for enjoyment, assured he'd found exactly what he wanted.

"They're good, aren't they?" a sultry female voice asked.

He looked up to see the blonde. He smiled at her, rose and motioned for her to take a seat. "Better than good. They're spectacular." He held out a hand before they sat down. "Nick Devlin."

She shook it and said, "Viv Renault. Luc's my husband."

"So you're here to offer moral support?"

"No." She dimpled. "I'm here because I like to hear them play."

Nick laughed. "Can't blame you there." They listened to the rest of the set in comfortable silence.

A short time later the set ended and Luc came to the table. Viv stood to greet him. He slid his arm around his wife's waist before saying to Nick, "Luc Renault. I see you've met my wife."

Nick nodded. "Just now. I enjoyed your set very much."

"Thanks." He looked at his wife, who winked at him.

Nick wondered what it would be like to have a woman share in your accomplishments. And your failures. He doubted he'd ever know. He felt a twinge of disappointment at that thought, but shook it off. Time to get down to business.

"We open a week from Friday. I'd like to sign you on as both the headliner for the grand opening and a regular in the months to come. We can talk terms and details now or later, if you want. The entertainment manager is around somewhere, I can page him. But we're prepared to top your most recent contract terms."

Luc wasn't quite successful at hiding his surprise, and his pleasure. "Mr. Devlin, it sounds like you have a deal," he said, stretching out a hand.

"Nick," he said as they shook hands. "Great to have you on board."

CHAPTER FIVE

TEN O'CLOCK THAT NIGHT, and Casey sat at the computer, staring at the spreadsheet and updating the data—in particular, the weather conditions and growth rate on the experimental hybrid crop.

After dinner she'd forced herself to change into shorts and tennis shoes and go back to the office, though in this miserable heat she'd much rather have skipped it to stay in the cooler big house. She hit another wrong key, swore, backed up and started again. After finishing the entry, she scowled and tipped her chair back, balancing with her foot on the desk.

The problem wasn't that she had too much work to do, or too little time to do it. No, the humiliating fact of the matter was that she couldn't concentrate because she kept thinking about Nick Devlin. What she couldn't figure out was, why?

She closed her eyes to consider that. He was good-looking, she'd give him that. Okay, more than just good-looking, he was as hot as they come. But

so what? She knew other men who were equally hot. Didn't she?

Irked at herself, she continued her catalog. He'd come along at a weak moment. At a time when she was seriously wondering if she'd ever find a man she wanted to go out with, never mind get serious about. And he was interesting. Intriguing. She wanted to know what was going on behind those amazing blue eyes of his, though she could hazard a guess about some of it. She wanted to know what he'd done, where he'd been. Obviously, he hadn't spent almost his entire life on a sugarcane plantation in Louisiana.

And whose fault is that? she asked herself. Though she'd had opportunities to travel, she'd turned most of them down. She'd always been too obsessed with the cane. So now, here she was, thirty-one years old, single and…feeling antsy. It was natural. She hadn't been close to a man since— Casey had to pause and think about that. It dawned on her with a sick feeling that she hadn't let a man near her—other than Murray, who was a friend and therefore didn't count—since her damn ex-fiancé had dumped her for another woman three years before.

"Looks like an uncomfortable place to take a nap," a deep, masculine voice said.

Casey's eyes flew open, the chair legs landed on

the floor with a thump and she stifled a shriek. Nick leaned negligently against the jamb. He filled the doorway, looking heart-stoppingly good in a short-sleeved white T-shirt with a faded logo that read *Margaritaville,* a pair of khaki shorts and Top-Siders.

"What's the matter with you?" she demanded, her pulse racing. "Are you trying to give me a heart attack, sneaking up on me like that?"

Without waiting for an invitation, he walked in. For a moment, he stood looking around. Casey refused to squirm, even though it more closely resembled the site of a tornado than an office. Papers spilled off her desk. Several days' worth of empty coffee cups sat on the desk and the floor. Files lay haphazardly on chairs. Filing wasn't her forte, either.

In one corner there was a large bag of fertilizer, papers stacked on top of it, waiting for Casey to decide whether to place a full order. Plaques from the LSU school of agriculture and the Sugar Coalition hung on the walls, several of them crooked. Tacked on the wall closest to the desk was an ancient poster from the New Orleans Jazzfest. Casey looked at it whenever she wanted to imagine getting away.

"Do come in," she said sarcastically.

"Thanks." He came all the way inside, leaned a

hip against a corner of her desk and smiled at her. "Pretty late to be working, isn't it? I saw the light and figured it was you."

"I have to do my paperwork at night." Casey made a frustrated motion at the computer, now blinking silently at her. "I hate computers."

"Really? I like them." She threw him a look of disgust and he continued. "Why don't you hire someone to take over those duties?" He glanced around the office and added, "And to file for you."

"Partly because it's an unnecessary cost, and partly because I'd have to train whoever we hired and I don't have the time." She thought about it a minute and added, "Besides, then I'd always have someone underfoot and asking me questions, which would drive me crazy."

"Are you saying you're antisocial?"

"Of course not. I like people fine." Most of the time. In small doses.

"Good. Then, why don't you come to the grand opening of the White Gold? As my date." She started to speak but he continued before she could. "Before you turn me down, I should tell you your friend Viv Renault said to tell you she was going to kick your butt if you didn't come." His lips curved into a smile. "Her husband's headlining the entertainment."

Casey sat up at that, so pleased for her friends

that she forgave him the ploy. ''You hired Luc's band?'' Viv and Luc had only recently gotten married, and Casey knew from Viv that her parents still hadn't totally accepted a son-in-law who happened to be a jazz musician and had to work for a living. This would infuriate them to no end. A huge smile spread across her face. ''Oh, this is great!''

He looked surprised. Then he leaned forward and twirled a stray piece of her hair around his finger, holding her gaze. ''So was the band,'' he said musingly. ''So, you'll come?''

She was torn. But at least if she accepted now, she could blame it partially on Viv. It had nothing to do with the shiver that ran up her spine as he pulled another strand of hair loose from her ponytail and toyed with it. ''All right. Knowing Viv, she will kick my butt. And it's just one date,'' she hastened to add, pulling away from him and brushing her hair back. ''No big deal.''

''Absolutely not,'' he agreed solemnly, but she saw his lips quiver.

He had a beautiful mouth. Masculine, but beautiful. Casey wondered what those lips would feel like on hers. Would he kiss soft, slow and lazy? Or would it be fast, hard and reckless? What would happen if she surprised him? If she leaned across the desk and pressed her lips to his? Their gazes locked. She had the feeling he knew exactly what

she'd been thinking. Hastily, she cleared her throat and averted her eyes.

"I had another reason for stopping by," he said.

Glad for the change of subject, she looked at him.

"I came to take you up on that offer."

"What offer?"

"You said when you had time, you'd tell me about farming."

"Farming? You want a lesson in farming? Now?" She really wished his voice didn't make her think of late nights and sin. Even asking a simple question about farming, he managed to put those images in her mind.

He shook his head. "Not a lesson. I want to know why you do it. And why you love it."

Taken aback, she thought about that. No one had ever asked her such a thing. She'd never met anyone who actually cared about her reasons for farming. The rest of her family were simply happy she liked it. Well, all of them except Aunt Esme. "I don't understand why you're interested."

"I told you." He tugged another strand of hair. "I like knowing about things."

"Stop playing with my hair," she said. She'd meant it to come out as a command, but her voice was entirely too husky, and the words sounded more like a plea.

''Does it bother you?'' he asked, but he released her hair.

''Yes. I get the feeling that's not all you'd like to be playing with,'' she said rashly.

His mouth curved upward but he didn't say anything. He picked up a paperweight—a rock she'd hurled at Jordan's head when he'd come to tell her he wasn't marrying her—and looked at it. ''I don't know many farmers. As a rule, they don't spend much time in casinos.''

''So the only people you know are gamblers?''

''Dodging the question?'' he asked. ''No, those aren't the only people I know. Still, if you look at life like I do, lots of people are gamblers who you might not classify that way. I mean, look at you. You gamble on whether your crop's coming in on time or some disaster will stop it. You gamble on what the yield will be. Whether there'll be a drought or too much rain. All sorts of things.''

''Nothing's a sure thing, is that it?'' she asked.

He smiled. ''What's the saying? Death and taxes are the only certain things in life.''

She stood, and so did he. ''Come on. I'm not sure I can explain my feelings very well with words. So I'm going to give you some hands-on experience in the life of a farmer.''

He looked a little wary. Casey laughed and strode

to the door. "Aren't you the one who's always looking for new experiences?"

"Depends on the experience," he said as he followed her out the door. *How bad could it be?* he asked himself, before another thought occurred to him. "I don't have to shovel sh—fertilizer or anything, do I?"

Casey cast a mischievous look over her shoulder. "Don't worry, I'll be gentle."

"Yeah, that's what I'm afraid of," he muttered.

Casey hopped in the ancient red pickup parked outside the greenhouse, barely waiting for him to get in before she took off down a dirt road that headed toward the cane fields. He knew that much from scouting out the plantation in the daylight. There was a partial moon, throwing off enough light that the night wasn't totally black—a good thing since the headlights had seen better days.

"This is my new hybrid field," Casey said, halting at a field that looked just like the others. She got out of the truck, motioning him to follow. "I told you about it the other night. LSU approved us to test a new cane."

The cane was tall, eight to ten feet, and the night was silent but for the leaves rustling in the breeze and the engine coughing in the background. An earthy scent permeated the air. "Is that a big deal? A new hybrid?"

She nodded. "Yes, it's quite an honor to be chosen." She glanced at the field again, then walked back to the truck. "But what I really want to show you is up ahead. To most people, a cane field is a cane field, so you'd be unlikely to notice the differences between them. I don't expect you to find this hybrid field fascinating, but I do."

She drove down the road, seeming not to mind the roughness that rattled his teeth, until they came to an unplanted field. This time she turned off the engine when they got out.

"Take off your shoes and socks," Casey said, and began taking her own off. "Come on."

Mystified, he did as she said. She took him by the hand and led him into the field. "This was plowed today. Luckily for us, it hasn't been fertilized yet." Once they reached the middle of the field, she stopped and dropped his hand. "Close your eyes."

"Why?" he asked suspiciously.

"Just do it. Close your eyes and wiggle your toes in the soil. Nothing else feels like fresh-plowed earth. Nothing else smells like it."

"I'm a lot more used to concrete beneath my feet than dirt." But it did feel good. Soft, sensual. A different experience, that's for sure.

"City boy, are you?" Her voice was soft and dreamy.

Nick opened his eyes and looked at her. "You could say that." He'd spent most of his childhood in Dallas, Texas. Since then, he'd been many places, but his business and interests took him to cities most of the time.

"I used to come out here when I was a little girl. Duke always told my mother if she couldn't find me, to check the fields." She opened her eyes. "I've wanted to farm since I was a child. It never occurred to me that my parents expected Jackson to take over that aspect of the plantation. Or that they thought I'd follow in my mother's footsteps. Instead, I dogged Duke's."

She sat down, crossing her legs tailor-fashion. Patting the dirt beside her, she said, "Here, have a seat. Or are you afraid of a little dirt?"

"I've gotten my hands dirty plenty of times," he told her as he sat.

"Really?" She looked him up and down. "You don't seem like the type."

"I could say the same about you. You're no typical Southern belle, are you, Casey?"

She smiled ruefully. "No, guess not. That's one reason Aunt Esme gets so put-out with me." Sighing, she rolled her head on her shoulders.

"My mother and Aunt Esme tried their best to get me to be like the other girls, but I wasn't happy unless I was following Duke around. The men

would talk sugar morning, noon and night. I loved it. Duke didn't especially like farming, but he's always had his hand in every aspect of the plantation. He was always more interested in the wheeling and dealing. Jackson seems to have inherited his talent for that.''

''What did you inherit? Since he didn't like farming?'' He tried to imagine being close to his parents, but since they'd dumped him when he was seven, that was impossible. Casey might as well have grown up on a whole other planet than the one he knew.

''His love of Bellefontaine, and the sugar business, I guess. I'm not like either of my parents. Not really. And especially not like my mother. Angelique is the epitome of a gracious Southern lady. Somehow I missed out on those qualities. I was a teenager before I realized most girls didn't spend all their free time eating, sleeping and breathing farming. I found out in a pretty brutal way that boys didn't appreciate a girl with no small talk except about sugar.'' She looked down at her chest. ''Not to mention, girls with no figure.''

He looked her over, half smiling. ''I'd say you filled out just fine.''

She shrugged. ''Maybe. But back then, I was gawky, awkward and had fallen desperately in love with the class president. He had a rep for dating only

cheerleaders. Which I wasn't. He nicknamed me Farmer and let everyone know that he wouldn't date me if my father paid him.'' A grin spread over her face. ''Jackson was a couple of years behind me, but he heard about it. He and some of his friends made sure the prez didn't repeat that. Or much of anything else for a few days.''

''Good for Jackson. So, did this guy break your heart?''

''No, only bruised it. He left the heartbreaking for my ex-fiancé, who didn't *quite* leave me at the altar.'' She pulled her knees up to her chin and wrapped her arms around them. ''Seems he found another woman who suited him better, and didn't want to tie himself up with me.''

''Suited him better?''

She glanced at him wryly. ''More money, higher social standing.''

''What a jerk.''

''In spades,'' she agreed, and laughed.

What kind of a fool would jilt a woman like Casey? ''I know what it's like not to fit in,'' he said after a pause, feeling an odd kinship with her.

''Do you?'' She tilted her head to look at him. ''Why didn't you fit in, Nick?''

''I grew up in an orphanage. From the time I was seven. Trust me, orphans fit in less than farmers.''

"I'm sorry. It must have been hard losing your parents so young."

"I didn't lose them," he said, already regretting ever speaking up. But he'd started it, so he might as well finish. "They dumped me."

She reached out and took his hand. "I'm sorry," she repeated, her voice gentle and sincere.

He shrugged it off, but he kept hold of her hand, rubbing his thumb over her knuckles. "It was a long time ago. I got over it."

"Meaning, you don't want to talk about your childhood."

"What's to talk about? It was lonely, not very pleasant, and I survived. Besides, most women aren't interested in my childhood."

"Why not? Hasn't anyone else ever asked you about your childhood?"

"You're the first." He smiled cynically. "The women I've known have been a lot more interested in the here and now. They don't care to hear about the struggle, they just like the results."

"What results?"

She scooted a little closer to him, looking at him as if she really wanted to know. Really wanted to know *him*. But that was an illusion. Nick had been proved right about too many women to trust one easily.

He turned his head to meet her gaze. "Money, sweetheart. That's what the women I know like."

"So, what, you're loaded?"

He grinned at her question. She didn't look particularly impressed. "I figured Jackson had told you."

"No." She dimpled. "We didn't talk about your money." She pressed a finger to her temple, as if thinking. "Let's see, how did he put it? Jackson said you had a reputation with women, and he was sure you deserved it."

"Who needs enemies when you have friends like that?"

"Hey, he's my brother. Annoying as he can be, he was just looking out for me."

"Can't blame him for that." He was honest enough with himself to admit that, and to realize he envied his friend the bond he had with his sister. Not that Nick was interested in Casey looking at him like a brother.

"Is it true?"

"More or less. I'm not innocent where women are concerned."

She snorted. "Now, that's something I'd never have guessed."

He grinned, then sobered. "But I don't lie. If I have a relationship with a woman, we both know the rules going in."

"Tell me, Nick, what are these rules?"

He leaned closer, until his mouth hovered near hers. "Why are you asking, Casey?"

"Curiosity?" she said, a little breathless. Her tongue slipped over her lips, moistening them.

"I think there's more to it than that," he said, and fitted his mouth over hers. Her lips parted, inviting him in, then her tongue touched his, a quick foray. He slid inside, but gently, not wanting to rush her, enjoying this first taste of her.

Pulling back was harder than he'd imagined. But he did, and waited for her to make the next move.

"More," she whispered, and kissed him.

Her arms came around his neck, her breasts settled against his chest, her mouth felt warm and sexy on his. Her tongue played with his, sliding against his in a way that made him want to do a lot more than just kiss her. He slipped his arms around her waist, ran a hand slowly up her back, to cup her nape beneath her ponytail.

She slanted her mouth over his as the kiss grew more urgent. Casey gave a breathy moan and nestled closer. He clasped her tight as they slid to the ground. He retained enough sense to make sure she was on top, but after that, all the sense he'd always assumed he had deserted him. His hands slipped over her rear, pressing her gently against him. She felt good, so damn good he didn't want it to end—

but what sanity remained told him she'd wake up to reality soon.

She drew back and stared down at him, her chest rising and falling rapidly. "That got out of hand. I didn't mean— I just intended to kiss you. Not crawl all over you."

"Believe it or not, Casey, that's all I intended, too."

She rolled off him and lay on her back in the dirt. He rolled to his side and looked at her. She started laughing.

"What's so funny?"

"What's funny is I believe you." She turned her head and smiled at him. "Tell me those rules of yours, Nick," she invited, that Southern Comfort voice tempting beyond belief.

He very nearly stuttered. He wasn't accustomed to a woman blowing him away, and Casey Fontaine certainly had. With nothing more than a kiss. Dangerous, that's what she was. His voice was gruffer than usual when he answered. "No promises. No expectations, beyond the present. No lies."

"So what's in it for either of us?"

"Fun."

"Fun? That's it, fun?" She turned on her side and rose on her elbow.

"Believe me, Casey, you and I could have a lot of fun together."

She stared at him for several moments, then leaned over and brushed her lips against his. "I'll think about it," she said.

And so would he. In fact, he suspected he'd think of very little else beyond getting Casey Fontaine into his bed.

CHAPTER SIX

NEITHER CASEY nor Nick spoke on the way back to the house. Casey pulled into the gravel drive at the back. She didn't know what to say to him. She was a little embarrassed, but more than that, she was still aroused. *Too bad,* she told herself. There was no way she intended to jump into bed with a man she'd only known a matter of days. Even if the idea did appeal to her senses.

"I should have driven to the *garçonnière,*" she said. "So you don't have to walk barefoot. There are stickers and fire ants between here and there."

"I put my shoes back on. A little dirt never hurt anything."

"A little dirt? We're *covered.* You might have shoes to spare, but I'm not ruining mine."

He got out and came around the truck. "What are you doing?" she asked when he opened her door.

He put his hands on her waist and hauled her out, into his arms. "Carrying you."

"You don't need to—" She broke off, clasping her arms around his neck as he began walking to-

ward the house. "At least let me get my shoes," she said, deciding not to fight. His mind was made up, and besides, she liked it.

She'd never been the kind of woman a man carried in his arms. But she didn't feel helpless. She felt empowered. And very, very female.

He went back to the truck and, somehow, they managed to get her shoes out without Nick dropping her on her head. They were both laughing by the time he started toward the house again. Still in his arms, she opened the screen door to the porch and Nick stepped inside with her.

"Thanks. You can put me down now."

"I could. Or I could walk back out the door and keep going until we come to the *garçonnière*." His voice rippled over her, a sexy caress in its own right.

She looked at his mouth, very near and very tempting. She shook her head regretfully. "Sorry. I'm not going to sleep with you tonight, Nick." He smiled. "What?"

"You said tonight."

"I did, didn't I."

As he set her on her feet, he let her slide against him. "Whatever you say," he murmured, and kissed her.

She didn't fight him, didn't resist the sizzle that started with her lips and spread throughout her body. Casey couldn't remember ever being kissed quite so

thoroughly. So…erotically. Her arms tightened around his neck as his hands slipped over her rear. He kissed her as if the slide of their lips, the tangle of their tongues was the only thing that mattered. A part of her wondered dimly why in the world she wouldn't go back to the *garçonnière* with him.

"Cassandra!"

It was a tribute to her aunt Esme's piercing voice that it only took two repetitions of her name to bring Casey out of the sensual fog in which she was swimming. She broke the kiss, drew back and looked up into Nick's smiling eyes.

"Thank God she doesn't have a shotgun," Nick said softly enough so only Casey could hear. "She looks mad enough to use it." He paused, then added, "I wonder if she'll sic her dog on me?"

Casey turned around. Her heart sank at the sight of Esme—and Toodles, quivering indignantly by her side. Esme's outraged expression promised the kind of scene Casey hated.

"What on earth is the meaning of this—this spectacle?" Her aunt stood with arms akimbo, eyes flashing furiously.

"Evening, Miss Esme," Nick said easily, fanning Esme's wrath.

She gave him a withering glare before returning to her niece. "Cassandra, I'm waiting for an explanation."

"You'd think I was thirteen, not thirty-one," Casey said. "The meaning is, I expect, pretty damn obvious." She turned around and started shoving Nick out the door.

"I've never run from a fight in my life, Casey," he said.

"This isn't your fight. It's mine. Go on. I'd rather deal with her alone. Please, Nick, just go," she added when he still hesitated.

"All right. I'll see you tomorrow." His hand slipped down her bare arm, a last caress. "Good night, Miss Esme," he added, shooting Casey a wicked smile.

Esme didn't bother to answer him. She remained standing, rigid with indignation. "I asked you a question, Cassandra, and I expect an answer."

"Aunt Esme," she said wearily, "I don't want to be rude, but this is really none of your business. For heaven's sake, I was kissing the man. It's not a big deal."

"I know what you were doing. I'm not blind and I'm not a dotard." She looked her niece up and down with distaste. "Obviously, you've forgotten you were raised a lady. You're covered in mud. Have you been rolling in the dirt with that man?"

"His name is Nick. And what I was doing is my own damn affair." Casey knew her voice was grow-

ing shrill, but she was exasperated almost beyond belief.

"Cassandra!" Esme put out a hand and tottered toward her. Casey thought it a bit much, considering she'd never in her life seen her aunt totter.

"You mean to tell me you're sleeping with that man? Why, you hardly know him."

"I'm fully aware of that. And no, I'm not sleeping with him. Not yet, anyway. But there's a very strong possibility I will be soon, so you'd better get used to the idea, Aunt Esme."

"Never!" Esme declared. "He's a gambler. A no-account gambler."

"He may be a gambler but he's not no-account. He happens to be loaded," Casey shot back, growing angrier by the minute. Not that his finances mattered to her, but she didn't like her aunt's judging him because of the work he chose to do.

Esme ignored that, sinking into a chair. "I could hardly believe my eyes. What if your niece had wandered in? What then?"

"Oh, don't be ridiculous. You're acting as if I was having sex on the table instead of simply kissing the man. I don't think Megan would be irreparably harmed by seeing me kiss someone."

"I might have known you'd make light of it."

"Yes, you should have. You know what, Aunt Esme, since I offend you so much I'll just make it

easy on you. I'll move into Wisteria Cottage tomorrow. It's almost ready, anyway.'' Her grandmother's cottage, two miles from the big house, had been unused since her death a few years before. A couple of months ago, Casey had decided to move there, and had been having it repaired.

"So now you're deserting us. What about the renovations to Bellefontaine? Have you even bothered to call someone in?''

"Of course I have. I'm meeting with Adam Ross tomorrow, as a matter of fact.''

Esme ignored that, lodging yet another complaint. "What about your niece? Don't you care about her?''

Casey gritted her teeth. "I'm not moving to the ends of the earth. I'll still be on the property, for Pete's sake. And I'll see Megan as much as she likes.'' She added tartly, "She does have a name, Aunt Esme. It's Megan. I suggest you use it.''

Esme flushed and started to speak, but apparently thought better of it. Ordinarily, Casey wouldn't have been so blunt, but when she lost her temper her mouth tended to run away with her.

"I should have expected it,'' Esme said heavily. "That man must have cast some kind of spell over you. I've never known you to be so reckless.''

"I haven't even begun to be reckless. Yet,'' Casey added. "Good night, Aunt Esme.'' She turned

on her heel and left her aunt alone with her righteous indignation.

EARLY THE NEXT MORNING, Casey met with Adam Ross. A good-looking man, Casey thought, with curling light-brown hair, blue eyes and a body that was obviously accustomed to physical labor. His muscles flexed as he pushed the stove aside to see the wall behind it. Definitely something to be said for construction work. More important than that, though, his credentials were excellent. Now she had to find out if he was affordable.

She drew in a breath, waiting for him to finish jotting down figures in a small spiral notebook. Nick had said Adam would give her a fair price, and she had to hope that was true.

Adam took out a calculator, punched in some numbers, then looked at her, his eyes twinkling. "Don't worry. Nobody's ever died of shock from one of my estimates." His lips twitched. "Of course, there's always a first time."

"Is it that bad?"

Adam glanced at the house, then back at her. "It won't be cheap because the materials aren't cheap. If you intend to pass the Historical Landmark inspection, then we have to use authentic materials."

Casey nodded. "I know. And we're on the tour

of historic homes, so there's no question of not do-ing it right.''

"The bad news is, the damage to the kitchen is pretty extensive. But the good news is, most of the damage is contained here, with only a little smoke damage to the adjoining rooms.''

"How much?'' Best get it over with.

He showed her his notebook. The materials esti-mate, which he'd noted wasn't complete, was high, but not a shock. However, his labor costs were far less than she'd expected. ''This can't be right. Shouldn't you charge more?''

He laughed. ''I'm not out to gouge anyone. This is a beautiful house and the job will look great added to my resume. I'm happy to have a bid on it.''

"Nick didn't twist your arm, did he?'' she asked, suddenly suspicious.

"Are you kidding? He knew I'd jump on some-thing like this.''

"Let's go outside,'' Casey said, walking toward the door. ''I still find it too depressing in here.''

Adam followed her out.

"You won't have a problem with the exterior, either?'' Casey asked.

Adam squinted at the charred wood. ''Shouldn't. I'll let you know if I run into any holdups.''

"Nick says he's known you since college.''

"That's right. We rented a house with a bunch of

other guys." He shoved the pencil behind his ear and smiled reminiscently. "Nick was the only one who'd help me with the repairs. Landlord gave us a break on the rent if we'd repair that house and his other rentals."

"I didn't know Nick could do construction."

"I think Nick's held almost every job there is. He put himself through school, worked two jobs to do it."

She suddenly realized that she'd been none-too-subtly pumping Adam for information about his friend. He was nice enough not to call her on it, but she glimpsed him hiding a smile. Clearing her throat, she said, "So, Adam, when can you start?"

"I can get a crew together and start next week."

Casey held out a hand and they shook on it. "It's a deal, then."

Adam smiled. "My pleasure."

LATE THE NEXT AFTERNOON, Casey took a break from work and went to Wisteria Cottage to see if her things had been moved yet. A couple of the part-time workers had promised to help her out when she'd asked first thing that morning. Last night, she'd stayed up into the wee hours, packing her clothes. Luckily, the workmen had almost finished the renovation, and her grandmother's furniture was still in place.

Casey loved the cottage and had looked forward to moving into it for a long time. She'd still be on Fontaine land, close to her cane fields and her family, and she'd have the privacy she craved. But she wished her departure from the big house hadn't been spurred by the fight with her aunt.

She had very fond memories of Wisteria Cottage, from visiting her father's mother as a child. Her grandmother had moved into it shortly after her husband's death. Though both Duke and Angelique had asked her to stay in the big house, Grandmère had insisted the big house only needed one mistress, and that was Angelique. Though fluent in English and French, she never spoke anything but French to her grandchildren, so Casey and Jackson grew up speaking both languages.

It wasn't a fancy place, or particularly large, but it was rather cozy. The exterior was whitewashed wood with brightly painted blue shutters, and front and back porches that ran the length of the building. A porch swing sat to one side of the front door. A woman seated on the swing waved and rose as Casey came up the steps.

"Hi, Viv. What are you doing here?" Casey asked, emerging from her friend's enthusiastic and expensively scented hug. As usual, Viv looked chic and classy in a sleeveless white linen dress that had undoubtedly come from Paris.

"Ah, *chére,* you look hot and tired already. You work far too hard," Viv said with a *tut-tut.* "I've come to see you, of course. The prodigal daughter— no, make that the prodigal niece." Viv followed her inside, talking a mile a minute. "So tell me, why did the dragon lady throw you out? Betty had to tell me where you were, since your auntie was too mad to be coherent."

Casey smiled at Viv's nickname for her aunt, one bestowed upon Esme when they were children. Esme hadn't been above holding Viv up to Casey as a prime example of proper Southern womanhood, but she'd never understood the bond between the two.

Viv, a slim blond beauty, was Casey's opposite in both looks and temperament. Whereas Casey's hot temper led her into trouble more than once, Viv rarely let go of her outward reserve. But Casey knew what went on beneath that finishing-school exterior. When given half a chance, Viv was a hellion, through and through.

A newlywed hellion. "Is the honeymoon over? I thought you couldn't tear yourself away from that handsome sax player you talked into marrying you."

"Why, *chère,*" Viv said, following her into the tiny kitchen. "I thought you knew better. I'm giving

him time to miss me." She smiled smugly. "The man's crazy about me, you know."

Casey smiled and nodded. "And you're crazy about him. Who'd have thought?" Casey opened the freezer door to turn on the ice-maker. "I have tap water and tap water. What would you like?"

"I'm fine. You go ahead."

Viv looked around and wrinkled her nose at the mess the workmen had left. A drop cloth covered one end of the living room floor, beautiful hardwood that ran throughout the house. Paint cans were everywhere, as were ladders. In place of a big ceiling fan that had once graced the living room, wires dangled, waiting for its replacement. "Couldn't you have waited until they were finished? Why the rush?"

Casey sipped her water and sat on the couch, an heirloom that had originally been covered in silk. However, since Jackson had spilled finger paint on it when he was five, it had been recovered in a more durable fabric. Viv took a seat in the French provincial chair next to it, crossing her legs and waiting for Casey to answer.

"Aunt Esme and I had a difference of opinion. I simply moved out a little earlier than I'd planned."

"And did this difference of opinion involve the oh-so-delectable Nick Devlin?"

Casey pursed her lips, considering whether or not

to lie. Viv knew her better than anyone else, though, so she might as well tell her friend the truth. ''Yes.''

''Well, don't stop there. I talked to Betty, remember? Did dragon lady walk in on you two doing the dirty?''

''Viv!'' Casey laughed out loud and shook her head. ''Of course not.''

''Humph.'' Viv frowned and crossed her arms. ''I want the whole story. And don't leave out any juicy details.''

''There aren't any to leave out.'' Except what happened in the field, and she didn't think Viv needed to know that. ''I was kissing Nick and Aunt Esme walked in and freaked out. You'd have thought we were having an orgy.''

''It does seem like a bit of an overreaction,'' Viv said. ''Are you sure that's all?''

Casey shrugged. ''Aunt Esme doesn't like Nick because he's brought another floating casino to town. She's completely irrational about that subject. Always has been and I've never figured out why.''

''You do seem to gravitate toward people your aunt doesn't like. Murray, me…now Nick.''

''Viv, she doesn't dislike you.'' She definitely disliked Murray, though.

''Dragon lady hasn't liked me since she caught us skinny-dipping in the fountain when we were fifteen.''

Casey choked on a laugh. "I'd forgotten about that. I think she was angrier about that than she was about last night. And that's saying something."

"I wonder what she'd have done if she'd known it was your idea?"

"Right now, she'd believe anything bad about me. She thinks I've lost all sense of propriety. Make that all sense, period."

"Have you?"

Casey thought about that, unable to keep from smiling. "Oh, no. I don't think so."

Viv stood. "Show me around. I haven't seen the place since your *grandmère* was alive. And while you do," she said, linking her arm through Casey's, "you can tell me what that cat-with-a-mouthful-of-feathers smile is all about."

Casey sighed and showed her the tiny guest bedroom with its adjacent bath. Then they walked down the hall, toward the master bedroom. "Grandmère's quilt," Casey said, opening the door and waving at the queen-size bed covered by a lovely quilt. "I found it in the attic. I dug some furniture out of the attic, too."

"Love the chaise longue," Viv said, running her hand over the antique chair. "It's a beautiful house, Casey. If I weren't so ecstatically happy, I'd be jealous." She sat on the bed and ran an appreciative hand over the fabric, her expression thoughtful.

"How do you like living at Luc's?" Casey sometimes wondered how Viv would adjust to Luc's cracker-box house in downtown Baton Rouge after living on her family's plantation for so long. The Pontiers owned one of the largest plantations on River Road, much bigger than Bellefontaine.

"It's a little cramped. We're looking for another place. A house." Her voice was dreamy, her eyes, when she glanced at Casey, even more so. "We're talking about getting pregnant."

Casey drew in her breath, a little surprised, though she didn't know why. Viv was her age, thirty-one, and married to a man she was madly in love with. "I don't think talking is how it happens."

Viv flashed her a smile. "Okay, Casey. You've avoided the question long enough. Who better to talk to about the new man in your life than your best friend? Spill. Now."

Casey sat on the chaise, kicked off her shoes and curled up comfortably. "He isn't the new man in my life."

"But you're thinking about it. And so is he."

Casey nodded. "I think I'm a novelty to him. He keeps saying he doesn't know many farmers."

Viv burst out laughing. "Casey, my poor deluded friend. He's not interested in your profession, you goose. You're beautiful. Don't let what happened with Jordan make you doubt that."

"Come on, Viv. We both know I'm no femme fatale." When Viv started to speak, she held up her hand. "And that's fine with me. I like who I am. Jordan didn't ruin that for me."

Viv muttered something that sounded like "lying, cheating son of a bitch."

"Forget about him. I have."

"Have you really? Truth."

"When I think about him at all, which is seldom, I'm so glad I didn't marry him. But just because I'm over him doesn't mean I'm ready to hop into bed with Nick Devlin." She closed her eyes and thought about kissing Nick. In the field, and again before Esme had interrupted them. Okay, so a part of her could have happily jumped into bed with him last night and never looked back. But she hadn't, which was probably a good thing. "It's moving too fast for me."

"You mean *he's* moving too fast."

"No." She shook her head. "It's definitely mutual." Casey thought about that a moment. "And he's so…so—" She broke off, trying to think how to describe him.

"Hot?" Viv said.

Casey laughed. "Oh yeah. Smokin'."

Viv touched a finger to her cheek as if seriously considering. "He's gorgeous…according to gossip,

loaded…and he has superb taste in music. What's not to like?''

''Nothing. But that's the thing, Viv. It's complicated. I mean, with him staying in the *garçonnière*. What if we have a one-night fling and hate each other?''

''That's simple. You kick him out. But I don't think that's going to happen.''

''I don't, either.'' No, she had a feeling the two of them together would be pure nitro. ''But what if it *is* great? Then everything becomes even more complicated.''

Viv got off the bed and walked to her. Putting a hand on her hip, she considered Casey. ''Why worry so much, *chère?* I think you've been way too serious for way too long. Besides, you never know what will happen. Look at Luc and me. We were supposed to have a one-night fling and never speak again. Look what happened with us. And we'd never have known if we hadn't taken a chance.''

''What happened to the cynical Viv I'm used to?''

Viv laughed. ''She fell in love and got married.''

I should be so lucky, Casey thought. No, she'd be much better off concentrating on having a good time with an intriguing man. Love wasn't likely to enter into the equation.

CHAPTER SEVEN

TWO DAYS LATER, Casey was still trying to unpack. Since she could only do it at night, it would take her awhile. But unpacking was much better than dealing with the computer. Tonight she'd decided to tackle her books. She had an eclectic collection, ranging from science fiction and romance to several nonfiction tomes on various aspects of farming. She'd also brought some of her well-loved childhood books. Someday she'd give them to Megan to read. She blew dust off *The Velveteen Rabbit* and placed it lovingly on the shelf. After staring at it a moment, she pulled it off and began to read.

When the doorbell rang a few minutes later, she was once again engrossed in the story of the stuffed rabbit who wanted to be real. Just as well, she thought as she answered the door. She needed to unpack, not read.

Nick stood on her doorstep holding the most gorgeous arrangement of flowers she'd ever seen. Roses, carnations, gladioli, lilies, as well as some others she didn't recognize.

"Housewarming," he said, handing her the vase.

"Thank you. Oh, Nick, they're beautiful." She buried her nose in the fragrant blossoms, more touched than she'd have believed possible. Men didn't give her flowers. Not even her fiancé had given her flowers. But Nick had.

He came in, shutting the door behind him. Casey took the flowers to the kitchen. "I'll knock them over if I put them in the other room," she explained. "I'm unpacking." And consequently, looked like hell. Just as she did almost every time she saw him. She resolved right then that when she went to the grand opening, she'd knock him dead.

"Viv told me you'd moved. Wasn't it kind of sudden?"

She walked into the den and took a seat on the couch, trying to think how to answer him. "No, it wasn't sudden. Just a little earlier than I'd planned."

He followed but didn't sit. Instead, he wandered around the room, looking at her bookshelves and what little she'd managed to unpack. He turned toward her. "That's not the whole story, though, is it?"

Casey sighed. "It was time for me to have my own place. That's all there is to it."

He looked at her speculatively, but he didn't belabor the point. There were boxes everywhere, and

she realized how little progress she'd made. She was tired of not being settled.

"Do you want me to go? Or can I do anything to help?"

She shook her head. She wanted to listen to his voice, that deep sexy sound that had intruded on her daydreams since the night she'd met him. "Thanks, but I needed a break, anyway. So tell me, how are things going at the casino?"

He took a seat beside her. "Pretty much as I expected. Everything that can go wrong has. It's always like that once you pick an opening date."

"Have you done this a lot? Opened casinos?"

He nodded, then stretched his arm along the back of the couch and began toying with her hair. "I've been doing it for about ten years."

"Is it always floating casinos?" she asked, trying to keep her mind on the conversation instead of leaning back into his touch.

"No. I've run them in Reno and Vegas. I opened one in Monaco once, and stayed to manage it for a while."

"Monaco. How fun." She'd been to France once, her only European excursion, but she hadn't made it to Monaco. Truthfully, though she'd enjoyed it, she'd been homesick. "Is it as pretty as its reputation?"

"Prettier." His hand slipped up to pull the clip out of her hair.

"What are you doing?" she asked breathlessly.

"Playing with your hair. Do you mind?"

"N-no." But he sure as shooting wasn't helping her think clearly.

"Good." He smiled and spread it over her shoulders. "You have seriously beautiful hair." He began to caress her neck with one hand, then eased her closer with the other. His lips brushed over her jaw, tempting her with kisses that stirred her to respond.

She turned her head and put her hand to his face, seeking his mouth. Nick's lips moved over hers, slowly and seductively. His tongue swept her mouth, once, twice. Again. Casey sighed and leaned into him. She threaded her fingers through the hair at his nape and let her mind empty of everything but the delicious sensation of kissing him.

He continued to kiss her, long drugging kisses. Her nipples tightened, aching. When he finally touched her breast, she couldn't stop a whimper of need. He cupped her breast, kneaded it gently through the fabric of her shirt. It felt good, especially since she wore no bra, but it wasn't enough. She wanted to feel his hand on her bare skin. Restlessly, she shifted and pressed her breast into his palm.

He took the hint. His mouth moved to the base

of her throat. He kissed her there, then murmured something against her skin. He slid her shirt up slowly, then palmed her bare breast. Casey closed her eyes and moaned. His fingers explored, then rolled her hardened nipples between them.

He returned to her mouth, and, almost before she knew it, she was lying on her back and he was between her legs as if he belonged there. She wrapped her arms around his neck and thrust her tongue in his mouth. His hips pushed against her and they both groaned. How could it feel so right when she'd only known him a matter of days?

Days. A little over a week. A small but insistent voice in her mind chanted *too fast, way too fast.* His lips fastened on her nipple and he sucked it. Her hands tightened convulsively on his shoulders and she wanted so much to ignore the reservations clamoring to be heard. If she meant to stop, it had to be now. She should have stopped him long ago.

"Nick." She pushed against his shoulders until he raised his head and looked at her. His eyes were dark and alive with desire.

"What's wrong?" he asked huskily.

"I'm not ready to—" She halted, then finished the sentence in a rush of words. "I'm not ready to make love with you. I know I should have told you before now, but I—" She broke off, unwilling to

admit she'd been too caught up in the moment to call a halt. "I'm sorry."

He pressed his mouth to hers, a gentle yet sensual flutter. "Does this mean that sometime you *are* going to be ready?"

Not trusting her voice, she nodded.

He smiled and kissed her again. "Good." He nibbled her ear, blew in it, and she shivered.

"I thought—" Casey sucked in a breath as his lips ran down her neck. "Oh, what are you doing?"

"Kissing you." He cupped her breast again, beneath the shirt she'd already pulled down. "You said you weren't ready to make love, but we can still kiss, can't we?"

"I'm pretty sure that's not all we're doing."

He laughed against her skin, then looked at her. "Relax, Casey. I won't push you into doing anything you don't want to do."

Why was she delaying the inevitable? Torturing them both, when all she had to do was take his hand and lead him to her bedroom.

The doorbell rang. "It must be a sign," she muttered.

"Are you going to answer that?" Nick asked when it rang again.

"I should." But she didn't want to. She didn't really want to move.

Nick got up, then reached out to help her. "I'll

go into the kitchen while you get that. Do you have anything to drink?''

''There are some diet drinks and milk in the fridge. Help yourself.'' She tucked her hair back in her clip and straightened her clothes, then opened the door, catching Murray just as he was about to pound on it.

''Murray, hi.'' He looked upset, so she added, ''Is something wrong?''

He looked her up and down, his face unsmiling. ''I need to talk to you, Casey. It's important.''

''It's not your father, is it?'' Roland hadn't been in the best health lately and she knew Murray had been worried about him. ''Is he all right?''

''He's fine. Are you going to let me in?''

''Sorry.'' She stepped back and let him enter, closing the door behind him. To Nick, who was still in the kitchen, she said, ''You and Murray have met, haven't you? The night of the fire?''

Nick came into the room and the two men shook hands and exchanged greetings.

''Sorry, I didn't realize you had company,'' Murray said.

Casey blinked at the blatant lie. Nick's car was parked in the driveway, and Murray knew very well it wasn't hers. ''What's up, Murray?''

Instead of looking at her, he looked at Nick. ''It's private.''

She was feeling more mystified by the minute. Especially when it became clear the two men were engaged in some silent communication.

Nick turned to her and smiled. "Casey, why don't you walk me out?"

"Now, wait just a damn minute. Nick, you don't have to leave."

"Don't worry about it. See you later," he said to Murray.

After another puzzled glance at Murray, she followed him. "Do you know what's going on?" she demanded as soon as they were outside. "Because I sure don't."

"Believe me, sweetheart, it's obvious." He put his hands in his pockets. "You didn't tell me you were tied up with someone."

"I'm not." She stared at him until it dawned on her what he meant. "You mean Murray? He's just a friend."

"Yeah?"

"Definitely."

"I don't think he's clear on that."

"Nick, Murray and I have never been anything but friends. He's my neighbor. We've known each other all our lives, went to high school together. It's crazy to think there's anything more than that between us."

He smiled and put his fingers beneath her chin.

"Tell me that after you've talked to him. I left my cell phone number on your kitchen counter." He dropped a kiss on her mouth and left.

She waited until he pulled out of the driveway before going back inside. Murray? Interested in her romantically? Nick had to be mistaken. It was just some weird guy thing.

She closed the door and glared at her friend, her irritation growing. "Was it really necessary to run off my company? What's so important?"

"Sit down, Casey."

He looked the same as he always had—brown hair, gray eyes, even features, medium build. A nice-looking man, though not astonishingly so. And Murray had been a good friend to her, especially after her fiancé jilted her. Remembering that, she relented a bit, and sat beside him on the couch. "What's wrong?"

"How involved are you with him?"

"With Nick? Is that what this is about? Why on earth is that any of your business?"

"Casey, please." He took her hand and squeezed it. "I need to know."

She sighed. "I don't understand any of this. I'm not involved with Nick. Exactly. But I probably will be before long. There, are you satisfied?"

He took both her hands and looked at her, more solemn than she could ever remember seeing him.

"After Jordan left, we had a lot of long talks. Do you remember when I told you he wasn't worth one of your tears?"

"Yes." Obviously, he was going somewhere, but for the life of her she couldn't see where.

"And that someday you'd find a man who would love you like you deserved to be loved?"

"Of course. And I remember not believing it. Then."

"Casey, I was hoping—I've hoped for a long time—that you'd let me be that man."

Her eyes widened. Murray was in love with her? "Murray, I—"

He interrupted. "No, let me finish. I've been in love with you for years. That's why I broke my engagement to Sarah. I knew I couldn't make her happy when I was in love with another woman. With you."

Casey shook her head, not wanting to hurt him. "Oh, Murray, I'm sorry. I always wondered what had gone wrong. You never would talk about it."

He looked impatient. "That isn't important now, but you and I are. I thought after Jordan you'd realize how I felt, and that you'd come to love me, too. But you never did. And I never pushed the issue because I believed you just weren't ready for another relationship. So I waited." He brought her

hands to his mouth and kissed them. "Then I heard about Nick Devlin."

"How did you hear? Because if you heard Aunt Esme ranting, you heard a lot of hooey."

"Is it? Then, what took you so long to answer the door?"

She gaped at him. "I cannot believe we're having this conversation. I don't have to answer to you, Murray. What I do isn't your concern. It never has been."

"It sure as hell is my concern. Am I supposed to stand by and let you become involved with another man? One who's bound to hurt you?"

She suppressed the flash of anger at his assumption she couldn't take care of herself. "You can't know that. You don't know anything about Nick."

"I know he's a player. He's going to break your heart and then move on. Just like Jordan."

"If he does, that's my business, isn't it?"

"Damn it!" He let go of her hands, sprang up and began pacing the room in agitation. "I'm not going to stand by and watch you ruin your life again."

"It's not your choice to make."

He pulled her up off the couch and into his arms. "Give me a chance, Casey. I swear, I'll make you happy."

Her mind reeled. If someone had told her half an

hour ago that she'd be standing here listening to a declaration of love from Murray, she'd have laughed. Before she could speak, he kissed her. She was so stunned, she simply stood there. She hadn't kissed Murray since they were kids, and never as he was trying to kiss her now.

She turned her head. "Stop it, Murray!" She twisted out of his arms and stared at him, chest heaving. "What's the matter with you?"

He dragged a hand through his hair, closed his eyes and shook his head. "I won't tell you I'm sorry. I should have done that years ago."

"If you had, it might have made tonight a little more comprehensible. You've never given me a clue that you were in love with me."

He laughed without humor. "Yes, I have. You just didn't want to see it. Think about it, Casey. What did I say after Jordan left?"

"That I could count on you," she said slowly, remembering. "That I could always count on you. But you didn't mean… You meant it as friendship."

"No. I was in love with you then. Just as I'm in love with you now."

He was in earnest. Whatever she believed, Murray believed he was in love with her.

"You know I care about you. I love you, but I'm not *in love* with you. And I never will be. I just don't feel that way about you, Murray."

"You might. If you'd allow yourself to think about it. All I'm asking is that you give us a chance."

She didn't want to lose his friendship. She had no desire to hurt him, either. But she saw no point in giving him hope when she knew for a fact she wouldn't change her mind. "I'm sorry," she whispered. "I can't."

He looked at her for what felt like a long moment. "There's nothing more to say, is there?" Then he turned his back and walked out the door.

Had she lost a friend, or would he get over it? His behavior had been so out of character. What had really happened to set him off? Had it been Nick...or something else?

WHEN HIS CELL PHONE RANG, Nick didn't need caller ID to know who it was. The timing was too perfect. "Hello, Casey."

"You were right."

Something else he'd been sure of. Murray had looked like he wanted to take Nick apart. It didn't take a genius to figure out why. But Nick wasn't certain of Casey's reaction. Had she told Murray to forget it, or had she decided to give him a chance? And if she had, where did that leave Nick? Why did it matter to him? He didn't plan to stick around Lou-

isiana forever. Why shouldn't Casey find happiness with a man who would?

"You sound upset. Are you all right?"

"No. Yes. Oh, I don't know." She sighed. "I'm a little freaked out. I had no idea he felt that way."

"But now you do. So, did you call me to tell me to forget it?" It shocked him to realize just how much he didn't want to hear that she'd decided she wanted Murray. Just how much he didn't want to envision Casey Fontaine with another man.

"Of course not." She sounded surprised. "I told you, Murray's a friend."

"Knowing how he feels might change your mind."

"It won't. Nick, what are you saying here? Have you changed *your* mind about—about us?"

"No way, sweetheart." Not a chance in hell. But he owed her honesty. "But I won't be here for long. If you think you could be happy with him—"

"I'm not good at games. Is this some clever way of dumping me? Before we even get started?"

"No. I was trying to be noble." Stupid idea, that.

Casey laughed. Nick liked her laugh. It was throaty and full and very sexy.

"Well, don't," she said. "Now can we talk about something else?"

"Sure. What do you want to talk about?" Nick

sat on the couch, picked up a glass of water and took a swallow.

"Oh, I don't know." She was silent for a moment, then said, "Phone sex."

He choked. "What did you say?"

She laughed. "Sorry, I just wanted to get your mind on something besides my problems with Murray."

"Honey, you sure as hell accomplished that."

She laughed again, husky, sexy, inviting. "Good. That was the idea." The smooth, whiskey sound of her voice was enticing as hell. He groaned and closed his eyes. "I could be over there in five minutes. No, make that three minutes."

"That sounds tempting," she said, her voice regretful.

"Tempting—but the answer is still no?"

She hesitated. "I wish...I'm just not used to moving this fast."

"I know." And he needed to back off. He wanted her intrigued, not frightened. He would survive. He could wait. Probably.

"Tell me something, Casey. Is your hair down?"

"What is this obsession you have with my hair?"

"I wouldn't call it an obsession. More like a fantasy. Is it down?"

"Yes. I don't sleep with it tied back."

He groaned silently, every muscle in his body

tightening at the image of her hair spread out over her shoulders, dark against the creamy skin.

"I have to admit, I have an obsession about you, too. Or a fantasy."

"You're killing me, Casey." And he had a feeling she damn well knew it.

"For me, it's your voice," she said, her own dreamy. "It's just so…luscious. So deep. Smooth. Rich. Sometimes I can almost feel it touching me."

It took some time before he could speak. "You're a very dangerous woman, Casey Fontaine." If she could turn him inside out over the phone, what would she be like in the flesh?

"Am I?" She sounded pleased.

"Trust me on this. You definitely are."

"Good. I like the sound of that. And Nick? I think you're dangerous, too."

He laughed. "Tell me more."

"You gave me flowers."

"That makes me dangerous?"

"I'm not a girly girl. Men don't give me flowers. But you knew. You knew exactly how to get to me."

"You may not be a girly girl, but believe me, Casey, you're all woman."

The question was, was he man enough to hang on to her?

CHAPTER EIGHT

IT WAS FUN, Casey discovered over the next few days, not to worry about the future. To take pleasure in the present. More fun than she'd had in a long, long time. Why shouldn't she enjoy herself with Nick? She was contemplating a fling, nothing more serious than that. Not every relationship had to have marriage in mind. Considering what had happened the last time she'd been serious about a man, she wasn't eager to try it again. Which made Nick perfect.

In the past week she'd only seen him once, very briefly. His time had been taken up with all the last-minute details of the upcoming opening. And since it was the beginning of the harvest, Casey had been unusually busy with the cane. Not to mention, she'd been keeping an eye on the renovations. Luckily for her, Adam was very capable and didn't need her butting into his business. His occasional questions weren't hard to handle.

Not so Aunt Esme. Casey had been avoiding her as much as possible, both because she didn't want

a lecture about Nick, and because every time she did see her aunt, Esme complained about the noise the workers made. Since Casey couldn't do a thing to change that, she figured the less she saw of Esme, the better.

But she and Nick had talked on the phone nightly, sometimes for hours. She figured the lack of sleep was a small price to pay.

Their conversations had covered every possible topic. Nick loved traveling and could tell stories for hours about the places he'd been. The people he'd met came alive for her when he talked. She'd never known a man with such a genius for meeting and describing interesting people. To someone who rarely left her hometown, it was fascinating. And so was he, she thought.

Oddly enough, her limited experience didn't seem to bore him. He asked her about the sugar industry, freely admitting he didn't know much, though Casey thought he knew more than most outsiders. He liked to ask her searching questions that made her really think about the answers.

Talking wasn't all he did. Every couple of days, she'd come home from work to a phone call asking if flowers could be delivered. The first time, he sent tiger lilies, bold, beautiful and exotic. The next time, two dozen long-stemmed white roses, every bloom exquisite. A variety of orchids came after that. At

night when she talked to him, she'd tell him to stop, but secretly, she couldn't wait to see what else he would send. She couldn't help but think of him, either, surrounded by the gorgeous colors and the delicious smells of the blooms.

It surprised her, how much she liked it. She was enchanted, to tell the truth. She'd never wanted to be treated like a Southern belle. The opposite, in fact. She'd gone out of her way to make sure everyone knew she was tough. She was Duke Fontaine's daughter, after all.

But Nick saw past all that, to the very feminine side of her that she sometimes forgot existed. For a woman who'd never really been romanced, it was a novel, and exciting, experience.

She answered the door late Wednesday afternoon to find yet another offering. This time, he'd given her a plant, a giant shell-pink ginger lily from Hawaii, the card said. It was breathtakingly lovely and, she suspected, rare. Her pleasure at the gift warred with her guilt over what he was spending on her. She didn't take time to read all the literature that came with it. Instead, she called Nick.

"Nick, are you crazy? This is costing you a fortune."

"Did you get the ginger lily?" he asked, sounding amused.

"I got it, all right. Nick, the deliveryman said it was shipped here directly from Hawaii."

"Yeah," he said, sounding distracted. "Hold on a minute." When he came back on the line he said, "It's amazing what you can find on the Internet. You can get flowers from all over the world."

All over the world? Good Lord, next he'd be sending stuff from Thailand or Madagascar or who knew what other exotic locale? Casey paced a few steps to look at the plant. Large pink shell-like blossoms grew on tall spikes. The leaves, pleated, soft and velvety, only added to the beauty.

"You can't keep doing this. I want you to stop."

"Why? Don't you like it?"

"Of course I like it! It's stunning. But you're spending too much money on me."

He chuckled at that. "Relax, Casey. I won't beggar myself sending you a few flowers."

A few flowers, she thought, glancing around at the vases sitting on every table, was the understatement of the decade. And now he'd started on plants. She looked at the ginger lily again, leaned closer to smell the blossoms, and nearly moaned at the luscious scent. Casey took a deep breath and confessed, "I can't grow plants."

"Of course you can grow plants. You're a farmer."

"I'm also a houseplant assassin. Ask anyone who

knows me. I even kill ivy. This thing is rare and exotic and needs special care. It won't last a day.''

"You're kidding, right?''

"Afraid not. Casey's black thumb is a running joke in the family.''

"Try keeping it in your greenhouse. That ought to be the ideal place for it." He paused, spoke to someone. "Sorry, I've got to go in a minute. A worker fell off a ladder and swears he broke his leg and is suing.''

"Oh, no. Go see about him.''

"I will, but I suspect he's faking it. One of the waitresses just told me she's seen him run this scam three times. He'll keep." He paused, then said, "Have lunch with me tomorrow. At Brew-Bachers.''

It would be hard to get away, but the local bar and grill was one of her favorite places. "It sounds tempting, but I'm not sure I can take off work.''

He made a smacking noise, and she laughed. "How can you turn down the best po'boys in Baton Rouge? Besides, I haven't seen you in days.''

To hell with it. She'd make time. "You're on. I'll meet you at noon.''

"Great. See you then.''

"Wait, before you go, Nick, have I thanked you for the plant?''

"No, you've been too busy yelling at me. And

Casey? Don't worry. If it dies I'll get you another one."

He hung up before she could respond.

BREW-BACHERS was a Baton Rouge institution. It wasn't much to look at, with red vinyl booths along the wall, red-and-white checked vinyl tablecloths and menus written on three big chalkboards hanging above the counter near the entrance. Baseballs lined a shelf behind the bar, and since football season had just started, a board with stats for Louisiana State University was also displayed. Everybody loved the place, from businessmen to the college crowd.

Nick was waiting outside when she arrived, standing beneath the red neon beer sign covering most of the window.

"Hi, I'm not late, am I?" she asked.

"No, I was early." He smiled and took her arm, holding open the door for her.

"You are a bad man, you know," she complained as they walked up to the counter to order. "All I thought about all morning was the shrimp po'boy. I'm starving."

Nick ordered a soft-shell crab po'boy and they took their drinks to a booth by the window. "I'm glad you came," he said. "I've been wanting to see you, but getting ready for the opening has been chaotic."

''I'm looking forward to tomorrow night.'' Which surprised her, because she'd never been much for parties. But then, she'd never had a date with Nick to a blowout like the White Gold opening promised to be.

''So am I.'' His gaze settled on her mouth and his eyes darkened. ''Very much.''

''I meant the opening,'' she said.

''I didn't.''

Her skin tingled as if he'd touched her. Their order number came up then and she sighed, regretting that the moment had passed.

Casey had just bitten into the crusty French hoagie when a rough voice said, ''Well if it isn't Ms. Bitch Fontaine. What brings you slummin'?''

Startled, she nearly dropped her sandwich. She glanced up to see one of her former employees glaring at her. Nick was halfway out of his chair and she put a hand on his arm to restrain him. ''I can handle this,'' she told him. ''What do you want, Broderick?''

''How 'bout a loan, Ms. Fontaine?'' he sneered. ''Since you took my job away from me.''

''You might try looking for another one,'' she said, unimpressed. ''And staying sober when you go to work.''

His face was mottled with fury. Before he could answer, Nick got up. ''I don't think the lady's in-

terested. But I'll be happy to take the conversation outside.''

Broderick's eyes lit up at the prospect of a fight. ''Yeah? You and who else?'' He added an obscene word.

Fortunately, the place was so loud and crowded, no one seemed to be paying them much attention. Casey stood up. ''Nobody's going anywhere, except you,'' she told Broderick. ''You need to leave.'' But she didn't expect him to go peacefully.

Casey saw the manager start toward them. Broderick must have decided he didn't want to take on two men, because he turned and left, though not before spitting out another obscenity.

''Nick, let him go,'' she said, and grabbed his arm. ''Just let him go. He's not worth it.''

His eyes were filled with anger. She sensed his struggle and kept her hand on his arm. ''Please?''

''You folks all right?'' the manager asked.

''Everything's fine,'' Casey said hastily. ''A little disagreement.''

''You should have let me break his face,'' Nick said after the manager walked away. ''Why does he have it in for you?''

Casey picked up her po'boy, though she'd lost her appetite. But she refused to let scum like Broderick ruin her day. ''He came to work drunk. Twice.'' She

shrugged. "So I fired him. He hasn't been happy with me ever since."

"Bastard. Let me know if he bothers you again."

"So you can get in a fight with him?" She shook her head. "I don't think so. But Nick—?" Their eyes met and she smiled. "Thanks for the thought."

CASEY HAD INTENDED to leave work early the following day in order to get ready for the opening. She started trying to go home around noon, but one thing after another required her attention and she didn't manage to get away until after six.

Casey had enough help that she could take a day off more often, but she didn't usually want to. Len Forsen, who'd given her her first tractor ride when she was a child, was perfectly capable of taking care of the farm. He'd been Duke's right-hand man, and was now hers. But like her father, Casey wanted to have her finger in all the Fontaine pies—or at least those concerning the growing of the cane.

Tonight, however, she intended to have a different kind of fun. She was going to a party. A party that, for once, she really wanted to attend.

Her doorbell rang as she was slipping diamond studs into her ears. Her parents had given her some beautiful pieces of jewelry, but Casey rarely wore any. Tonight's affair was formal, though, so she'd

dusted off the studs and matching diamond-drop necklace to go with her dress.

Fortunately, she'd had just the thing—a dress she'd bought to wear to a formal dance with Jordan. Casey hadn't wanted to go, which was yet another thing they'd fought about, but she'd let him have his way. At the time she hadn't known that his affair with their hostess—the same woman he'd later dumped Casey for—was the reason he'd insisted on attending.

Viv all but danced inside when Casey opened the door. "You are not going to regret letting Nick send that limo for us," Viv said. "I already had a glass of champagne on the way to your place."

Casey laughed. "Now, why does that not surprise me? And if I hadn't relented, you'd still be nagging me." Her friend looked striking, as she always did, her cool beauty enhanced by the flowing white gown.

"Damn right, I would." Viv looked around and then gave a long whistle. "Wow."

"It's a bit overwhelming, isn't it?"

"Spectacular," Viv agreed, nodding. "It looks like a tropical rain forest in here. That man really knows how to charm a woman."

"You're not kidding. I told him no one ever gave me flowers and, well—" she gestured around the room "—this is the result."

Beside the door sat the latest offering, a mixed arrangement of Hawaiian gingers, heliconia, and anthuriums, all in varying shades of red. "These came today." She looked at her friend suspiciously. "Did you tell him I was wearing red?"

Viv shook her head. "Maybe he's a mind reader."

"Sometimes I think he is," Casey said slowly. "A man who knows women that well is scary."

"And exciting. Isn't that part of the thrill?"

Casey laughed again. "I guess so," she admitted. "But I can't help wondering if I'm getting in over my head here. I've never met anyone like him before."

"Relax," Viv said, linking arms with her. "Nick Devlin's exactly what you need right now. He's a great guy who obviously knows how to show a woman a good time. What are you so worried about?"

"I'm not worried," she said automatically.

Viv lifted an eyebrow skeptically and tugged her out the door. "Good, let's go, then."

But she *was* worried, Casey realized. Worried that she would wind up liking Nick Devlin too much for her own good. In fact, she already did.

NICK ENJOYED a lot of things about a new casino, but opening night was always the biggest kick for

him. By now, the managers were in place, and his main job was to talk to people.

He glanced around, satisfied that the decor was opulent without being tacky. As he'd intended, the glass chandeliers, long gilded mirrors and plush velvet hangings harkened back to an earlier age, when riverboats plied the Mississippi and Mark Twain was writing.

The first floor was the heart of the casino. It hadn't yet reached the din that would soon be constant. Still, the early arrivals were already lined up at the slots and tables. Bells whistled, coins clinked, chips rattled, and people shouted from the craps table when someone hit big—or lost.

Nick liked the noise. Oh, not as a regular diet, but he enjoyed the sounds of people having a good time, of money changing hands and of the excitement of patrons placing bets and winning. And he didn't have to be the one gambling to enjoy it. Most of the time, it was enough just being a part of it.

He sometimes wondered if his pleasure in the atmosphere had something to do with the orphanage where he'd spent eight long years—a cold, dismal place of hushed tones and grim children. Any time the kids rebelled, the rules became even more restrictive. Nick had left at fifteen and never looked back.

While he was waiting for Casey to arrive, he met up with Adam, who wasn't much on gambling or parties but had agreed to come. Nick figured his friend would enjoy himself. Adam liked food, women and music, and there were plenty of all three at the White Gold tonight.

"Great place, Nick," Adam said after they'd shaken hands.

"Glad you made it."

"Wouldn't miss it." He glanced around, taking in the decor. "Some boat."

"Thanks. I think Moreau is satisfied." If the man couldn't make a success out of the place after this opening, then he was incompetent. Nick had some concerns about Moreau. The guy had been a little flaky lately, but nothing so drastic as to really worry Nick. Still, the man was here tonight and was taking on his responsibilities as host. Nick had seen him last on the third level, where the high rollers hung out. Nick felt sure, though, that any problems tonight would be strictly his to solve.

"I've been meaning to tell you, thanks for recommending me for the Bellefontaine job."

"No problem. Besides, you already thanked me."

"It's a great job. Casey's a pleasure to work

for. Not to mention," he added with a smile, "to look at."

Nick shot him a sharp glance, surprised at the twinge of jealousy he felt. He'd never been jealous before. What was different about this time? "Yeah, she sure is. And Adam?" He waited until Adam met his eyes. "Looking's all you'd better do."

Adam laughed. "Had that figured out already."

Nick didn't care for the fact that he'd been so easy to read, but since Adam was one of his oldest friends, he shrugged it off.

"Is the food any good?" Adam asked.

"It better be," Nick said, thinking of the small fortune they'd been forced to pay the head chef. "There's a buffet on the second floor. With everything from Cajun to Continental. A jazz band is playing later tonight. They're good."

"Sounds great. I'm starved." Adam stared over Nick's left shoulder.

"Wow," he said reverently.

Nick turned around and saw Casey and Viv. One brunette, one blonde, both perfect. Viv waved at him, then headed toward the dining room where her husband was setting up. A smile tugged at his mouth. "I'll second that."

As she reached him, Casey put her hands in his and kissed his cheek. "Nick, the place is gorgeous."

"So are you," he said truthfully. She looked and smelled like a million bucks. Dressed in jeans or shorts, Casey was a remarkably pretty woman. Tonight, she was a knockout. Her dress was red, slinky and provocative, hugging her curves closely. The sparkly material shimmered when she moved, and skinny straps held up a low-cut bodice. It was a beautiful dress, and sexy. And to top it off, she'd left her hair down. Deep auburn highlights glinted in the rich brown that fell in long waves past her shoulders. Nick was finding it hard to breathe, much less talk coherently.

They stared at each other, oblivious to their surroundings. Adam cleared his throat. "Hello, Casey."

Her hands still in Nick's, she blinked, then turned to look at Adam. "Oh, Adam. Hi. I didn't realize that was you standing there."

"Don't I know it," he said ruefully. He punched Nick lightly in the arm. "Lucky devil," he muttered. "Since I'm obviously superfluous here, I'm going to scout out the food."

"Yeah, later," Nick said, still gazing at Casey.

"We were rude," she said, after Adam left.

"Probably." Not that he cared. Right then, all he cared about was looking at her. "He'll get over it."

"Still. I should—" She broke off as he touched her face with one hand.

He stroked her jaw, marveling at how soft and smooth her skin was. If they were alone he'd be tasting that luscious skin right now. "Should what?"

She shook her head, her eyes dazed. "What were we talking about?"

"You keep staring at me like that and we won't be at the party for long." He wanted to take her to a nice, private place and make mind-blowing love to her. And then he wanted to do it all over again.

She moistened her lips, making them slick, inviting, and as red as her dress. It was all he could do not to lean down and kiss her, but he knew if he did, he wouldn't want to stop.

"That sounds…tempting. But don't you have responsibilities here? You can't just up and leave, can you?"

"No, I can't. Not yet. But the party's officially over at midnight." He brought her hand to his lips and kissed it. "And then all bets are off."

"Midnight," she said. "Just like Cinderella. I hope I don't turn into a pumpkin."

Nick laughed. "It was her coach that turned into a pumpkin. And you're more beautiful than Cinderella ever thought of being." He smiled as delicate

color suffused her face. ''Come on.'' He took her hand and placed it on the crook of his elbow. ''Let's go get you something to eat. I'm sure there are some people in the dining room I should be talking to.'' And maybe, just maybe, if they weren't alone, he could manage to keep his hands off her until midnight.

On their way to the dining room, they ran into Hank Jensen, the Fire Inspector. Nick cursed himself for inviting the man. The last thing he wanted was for Casey to think about the fire, or anything that would upset her. But she was already stopping and shaking hands with Jensen before Nick could steer her away.

''Have you found anything out about the fire?''

Jensen nodded. ''Not as much as we'd like. And unfortunately, nothing that will lead to an arrest. I'm sorry, Casey, I'll let you know as soon as we turn up anything definite.''

He said goodbye and went on his way, leaving Casey staring after him with a frown.

''Give them some time,'' Nick said. ''I'm sure these investigations take longer than we can imagine.''

She glanced at him. ''Apparently so. But in the meantime, someone is running around thinking he got away with arson. Who knows if he'll try again?''

''Casey,'' he began, wanting to soothe but not really knowing how.

With a visible effort, she shook off her mood and smiled at him. ''No, it's okay. There's nothing I can do about it, after all. Why don't you show me around?''

''Why don't I?'' he said.

His feelings had started to worry him. He'd never before had such a need to protect a woman, to see that she wasn't hurt. Why Casey, and why now?

CHAPTER NINE

LATE IN THE EVENING, Nick had to take care of a problem with the dessert chef. When he returned, he couldn't find Casey anywhere. He had almost decided she'd had the limo driver take her home when he spied Viv, playing a slot machine while her husband looked on.

They made an interesting pair, with Viv so fair and Luc so dark. Though the band had long since packed up for the evening, Luc and Viv had stayed at the party at Nick's invitation. Nick noticed they seemed a lot more interested in each other than in feeding coins into the machine.

"Have you seen Casey?" he asked Viv when he reached them.

"Not recently. Why, has she disappeared?"

Nick nodded. "I had to take care of some business, and the next thing I knew, she'd vanished. I thought she might be with you, but obviously not."

"Try the deck," Viv said. "Casey's not big on crowds. She probably went out there to catch some fresh air."

"Thanks, I'll do that." Sure enough, he found her outside on the second deck. Alone, but she didn't appear lonely. She was leaning against the railing, facing the river, with her head tilted back and her eyes closed. The wind ruffled her hair and pressed her dress close to her body. He wondered if she'd worn that dress knowing it was designed to make a man sweat. It was sure succeeding with him.

"Hey, I thought you'd run out on me."

She turned, and her smile was easy and inviting. "No, I'm just enjoying the night. Listening to the river."

"It's pretty, isn't it?" He propped his arms on the rail beside her. "Imagine the stories this river could tell."

"All about the people who traveled it—from gamblers, to pirates, to runaway slaves," Casey agreed. "Some of them have had their stories told. Some never will."

They were quiet for a moment. The moon shone, a bright strip of light that illuminated the water. Waves lapped quietly against the boat, the noise of the casino behind them muted. The breeze was gentle but steady, and smelled of water and the faint scent of Casey's perfume. His stomach clenched, desire rising in his bloodstream. *Not yet,* he told himself. *Not yet.*

"Crowds get to me after a while," Casey said.

"I'm not used to being crammed into one place with so many people." She laughed. "I need my space, I guess." Glancing at him, she added, "But crowds don't seem to bother you. I watched you, working the room. People like to talk to you."

That was true, he supposed. "I enjoy them." Usually.

Unless he wanted to get a woman alone. Get Casey alone. And naked.

"They enjoy you, too. Especially the women." She reached up and tweaked his bow tie. "There's something about a good-looking man wearing a tux that makes women's hearts go pitter-patter."

"Yeah?" He put his arms around her waist. "What about your heart, Casey? What is it doing right now?"

She slid her hands up the lapels of his coat, then linked them behind his neck. "Galloping," she said, that aged-whiskey voice of hers as tempting and sultry as the Louisiana night.

He kissed her, as he'd been wanting to do all evening. Deep and hot and long.

She wrapped her arms tightly around him and kissed him back, her soft breasts pressing against his chest, her body warm and supple. His hands slipped down to cup her buttocks and urge her close against his hardness, against the ache.

He skimmed his lips over the pulse at her neck. "I want to make love to you, Casey."

"I know." Her breathing faltered when he pushed against her. "I want you, too."

The words he'd been waiting to hear. He pulled back enough to look in her eyes. "You're sure?"

She said nothing, but nodded, her eyes dark and alive with passion.

"Think you're too good for my boy, do you?"

At the slurred words, Nick and Casey both turned. Roland Dewalt stood a short distance away, none too steady on his feet.

"Roland?" Casey said. "What are you—"

He interrupted, jabbing a finger in her direction. "You think you're too good for a Dewalt, but you're taking up with this gutter rat. You're nothing but a little slut. Murray's lucky—"

He broke off as Nick grabbed him by the shirt front and shook him. "Keep your drunken ramblings to yourself, Dewalt. Neither the lady nor I have any use for them."

Dewalt sputtered but subsided, fear lighting his eyes. And it should. If he hadn't been thirty or more years older than Nick, he'd be lying flat on his back right now.

Fortunately one of the security guards who must have heard the scuffle walked up, and Nick was able to hand the older man over. "Escort him off the

boat,'' Nick told the guard, wiping his hands distastefully. To Dewalt he said, ''The White Gold can do without your business in the future, Dewalt. Don't come back.''

Nick turned to Casey, unsure what to say. She wasn't looking at him, but stared out across the water, arms crossed protectively over her chest. ''I've never liked him much,'' she said after a moment. ''He's always been hard on Murray. An unforgiving and demanding kind of man. But I didn't realize until now how much he disliked me.''

''Sounds like he was just mad because you turned down his son.'' He put his arm around her and hugged her. ''Don't let him ruin your evening.''

''He couldn't do that. Still, it's not very pleasant being called a slut.''

Nick's arm tightened around her. ''I'm sorry. I wish I could have stopped him sooner.''

Casey shrugged. ''I'll survive. I wonder why Murray told him about what happened? They're not at all close, but it's pretty obvious Murray must have said something.''

''Could be the old man caught him at a weak moment. Forget him.'' He kissed her, but briefly. ''Let me take you home.'' He kissed her again, more deeply this time. ''Be with you. Make love to you. What do you say, Casey, will you let me do that?''

She gazed at him, then smiled, slow and sweet.

"Yes." She pressed her lips against his. "Take me home, Nick."

SOMEONE HAD TAUGHT Nick Devlin manners, Casey reflected, as he took the key from her and opened the door to her house. He hadn't let her open a door or get a drink for herself all night. Not that she minded, she simply wasn't accustomed to being treated quite so courteously. He pushed open the door, and she walked inside and halted, staring at a scene set for romance.

The lights were dim and the music low, a background thrum of soft, sexy guitar concertos. A bottle of champagne was chilling in a silver ice bucket next to the couch. On the coffee table, which was covered with a fine white cloth, were two crystal champagne flutes, a crystal bowl filled with strawberries and a silver chafing dish filled with chocolate sauce. A vase of roses—new ones—sat in the center of the low table. Candles were placed in strategic locations around the room, and the air was filled with the scent of a hundred flowers.

She couldn't say a word as she watched Nick light the candles. She'd read about such scenes, had seen them in movies, and secretly wondered what it would be like to have a man go to such enormous trouble for her, though she'd never imagined it would happen.

It was wonderful. For the first time in her life she felt absolutely special to a man. Finally, she found her voice. "How did you manage this?"

His mouth curved. Those lovely, skillful lips that she knew for a certainty would soon be spreading kisses over her skin. A shiver of anticipation shot up her spine.

"Betty helped me set it up."

"Betty?" She blinked as he popped the cork and poured sparkling liquid into the glasses. "Our Betty? She doesn't have a romantic bone in her body."

"*Au contraire.* Betty is the soul of romance." He smiled and handed her a glass. Though he'd left his coat, vest and tie in the car, his white shirt was a beautiful contrast to his black hair, tanned skin and those Irish blue eyes. "Truthfully, though, I'm not sure whether she did it because she felt sorry for a poor, lovesick man, or because she knew it would royally tick off your aunt when she found out about it."

The thought had her smiling. "I'm having a hard time seeing you as lovesick." She, on the other hand, was coming dangerously close to tumbling madly in love. Not a wise thing to do, but at this point almost inevitable. "Besides, I'm not really the type to inspire flights of...passion." Or so other men had told her often enough.

"Who said that, Casey?"

She shrugged. "No one important."

"To us," he said simply, clinking his glass to hers.

She tasted the champagne, sighing with pleasure as the bubbles of flavor exploded on her tongue. "I thought I wasn't a champagne sort of woman, but I was wrong."

"You're wrong about something else, too," he said.

She could feel his gaze on her as if he'd caressed her. It made her want to rip off her clothes and beg him to have his way with her. *How did a man seduce you simply with his eyes?* "What?" she whispered.

He set down his glass, then took hers and set it beside his. He plucked a rose from the vase and twirled the stem through his long fingers. "You dazzle me, Casey."

"D-dazzle? M-me?"

He stroked her cheek with the petals of the rose. "Yes, dazzle," he repeated. "It makes me want to pamper you." With a featherlight touch, he slid the rose down her neck. "Romance you," he murmured, his voice husky and deep. The rose skimmed to her shoulder, ran down the length of her arm. "Seduce you."

Suddenly dizzy, she closed her eyes. "You're succeeding."

He laughed softly and moved closer. "Good. Do you know what this rose is called?"

She opened her eyes and looked at it. The heart was closed tightly, the petals a pale, pearl pink. As the petals unfurled they faded from pink to a whisper of yellow. "Gorgeous?"

"It's called Rapture," he said, and kissed her.

She was bewitched, she thought as his lips covered hers. In totally over her head, and she couldn't bring herself to care.

His hands were buried in her hair. He tasted her as if she were champagne, tilting her head back to increase his access. Then he pushed the strap off her shoulder and caressed it slowly, before his mouth replaced his hand.

Casey leaned back and moaned as his tongue traced slow circles on her shoulder and down to the swell of her breasts. "Nick, take me to bed." Another thirty seconds and she'd be begging.

"I will," he murmured. "I want to kiss you all night. Right here," he said, and placed his lips between her breasts. "You smell like flowers. Like roses."

"Perfume. Passion rose," she managed to say, her fingers clutching his head.

She felt him chuckle, then his hands slipped be-

neath the fabric of her dress to her bare flesh. Her fingers tightened on his shirt. "Take this off."

He shed his cummerbund and tugged his shirttail out of his pants, but then he stopped. "Unbutton it," he said softly.

Casey did, before spreading the shirt wide and placing her hand over his heart. It beat strong, steady. He pulled the shirt off the rest of the way, letting it drop to the floor. She slid her hand across his chest, tangling her fingers in the sprinkling of dark hair, then moving down to the tight muscles of his stomach. He sucked in a breath when she paused, let out a groan when she dipped farther down and covered his erection.

"Casey," he said, his voice a warning growl.

She met his eyes but continued stroking him, reveling in the feeling of power it gave her. "What?"

"My turn."

Reluctantly, she withdrew her hand. She turned around, drawing her hair over her shoulder, out of his way. The zipper glided down, then he pushed the dress down her body until it pooled at her feet. She stood with her back to him, wearing a red strapless bra, tiny panties and thigh-high hose. She started to step out of her dress and heels, but he stopped her.

"Wait."

She looked over her shoulder at him. "Nick, what are you doing?"

His eyes were intense when he raised them to hers. "Admiring perfection."

"Can you do it a little faster?"

He laughed. "Yeah, I can do that." He swung her up in his arms and started toward the bedroom.

Casey kicked her shoes off, dropping one in the hallway, one in the bedroom doorway. With one hand, he pulled the covers back, then placed her on the bed with a hastily uttered, "Don't move."

He pulled a handful of Mylar packets from his pocket and tossed them on the bedside table, then started to strip off the rest of his clothes. She rose on her elbows and watched every move, how his chest and arm muscles rippled, how his erection jutted out defiantly. Her only thought was having him inside her.

Then he was on the bed, kissing his way down each leg as he peeled off her panties and hose. He removed her bra and caressed her breasts, sucking them until he had her panting.

"Nick, now," she said, gasping.

He reached for a packet, ripped it open and covered himself. Then he kissed her mouth and entered her, thrusting deeply. He pulled back and with a slow revolution of his hips, moved inside her again. Casey bit her lip, nearly screaming at the intense

pleasure. He pulled out and entered her again and again. This time she did scream, but it was lost as his mouth came down on hers.

He lifted his head and their eyes met. He gave a final push, and his body stiffened as he emptied himself with a guttural cry before collapsing on top of her.

He should have been too heavy, but she liked the weight. Her mind drifted as she felt him press kisses into her neck. Her body felt boneless, and she was so satisfied she could have purred.

Nick looked down at her as he propped himself on his arms. He didn't speak, he just searched her eyes. What he expected to find, she couldn't imagine.

"Nick? Is something wrong?"

He shook his head slowly, then smiled, bent his head and touched his lips to hers. "No, nothing. In fact—" he kissed her again "—everything is very, very good."

SOME TIME LATER, Nick went into the living room to get the champagne and strawberries. He glanced around, enjoying the scene—the food, the wine, the candles burning. Not eager to burn the house down, he snuffed them out, one by one. A scene of seduction, but had he been the seducer or the seduced? He sat on the couch, needing a moment alone, a

moment to think without Casey bombarding his senses.

Troubled, he shook his head to clear his mind. What had nearly happened in there? He'd come within a breath of telling Casey he loved her. Which couldn't be happening. He couldn't be falling in love with her. He didn't do love, didn't know anything about it. Casey was beautiful and sexy, and he enjoyed being with her. But love her? He'd been feeling the aftereffects of great sex, that was all.

And she was waiting for him. Naked and beautiful, so why was he wasting time alone? He stacked the bowl of chocolate sauce on top of the strawberries, and picked up the bottle of champagne.

When he returned to the bedroom, Casey had pulled the sheet over her breasts and was lying on her side. Her hair spilled over the white sheets in a riotous mass, her eyes were deep green pools, still slumberous. And her mouth, Lord, her mouth was still swollen from their lovemaking, full and pouty and luscious. He wanted to sink into her, all over again. It had been a long time since he'd seen quite so tempting a sight. If ever.

They fed each other the strawberries dipped in chocolate, laughing and exchanging kisses as the juice dribbled down their chins.

"I have a confession to make," she said. "I've never done this before."

He knew she didn't mean making love.

"You know, eat strawberries and drink champagne in bed," she said when he didn't respond.

"We haven't had any champagne yet," he reminded her. "Not in bed, anyway."

"Have you?"

He didn't pretend to misunderstand her. "Are you sure you want the answer to that?"

She gazed into his eyes, hers crowded with conflicting emotions. "Yes."

"The truth is," he said slowly, choosing a piece of fruit and handing it to her. "I don't remember."

"Why?" she asked, her voice husky.

"Because right now, the only woman I see is you." He leaned over and kissed her, tasting the fruity sweetness and her own unique taste beneath it. Spicy. Exotic. Casey. "The only woman I want is you."

Their gazes locked, she sucked in a breath. Then she smiled, a flash of daybreak. "Maybe I'm a fool, but—" she fed him a strawberry "—I believe you."

"You're not a fool, Casey." He twined his hand in her hair, pulled her forward to meet his mouth. "How about that champagne?" he asked, long moments later.

"You didn't bring any glasses."

He smiled. "I know." He pulled the sheet off her and reached for the bottle. He poured champagne

directly into her mouth until she sputtered and laughed, then he tilted the bottle again and watched a thin stream trickle over her breast. ''This is the best way to drink champagne,'' he said, and traced the path of the liquid with his tongue.

Casey gasped and arched her back. ''That feels good. Wickedly good.''

''That's the point,'' he murmured, and lost himself in her.

CHAPTER TEN

THE PHONE RANG, shrill and insistent. Casey cracked open an eye. The clock read 6:24 a.m. Since she'd had only three hours sleep, she closed her eye and rolled over, ignoring the sound. After a while it stopped, but then started again minutes later.

She snatched up the phone. "What? And this better be good."

"Casey, it's Len."

"Len?" She sank back on the pillows. Len, her foreman. Her sleep-deprived brain finally made the connection. "What's wrong? I told you I'd be in late today, didn't I?"

"You did," he said grimly.

Casey glanced at Nick, saw his eyes were open and watching her. He looked so good, with stubble shading his jaw and his black hair tumbled from both sleep and her fingers. Then he smiled at her and her synapses misfired.

"Casey, did you hear me?"

She dragged her gaze away from Nick and tried

to focus on Len. He wouldn't have called if it wasn't important. "I'm sorry. What did you say?"

"I asked if you sent the harvester in for repairs and forgot to tell me."

Nick's hand covered her knee. She ignored it, or tried. "The harvester? Why, is it broken?" How could it be broken? They'd bought it earlier this season.

He swore, which told her how serious this situation was. Len never cursed in front of her, though when he didn't realize she was around, she'd heard him blister the ears of others unlucky enough to incur his wrath.

"It's gone," he said.

"Gone?" she repeated blankly. She sat up abruptly and swung her legs over the side of the bed, her back to Nick. "The harvester is gone?"

"I went to the field where I left it yesterday and it wasn't there. I figured maybe you'd moved it into the barn. Casey, I've looked in every field and building it could fit in. It's not here. It's not on Fontaine land at all."

She sprang up and began to pace. "You're telling me a machine the size of a small house vanished? Overnight? Without a trace? That's impossible."

"Tell me about it. Do you want to call the police or do you want me to?"

She pressed her fingers to her temples, trying to

think. "You do it. You know more than me at this point, anyway. I'll get dressed and be in the office in twenty minutes. I'll start the calls to borrow a harvester, too. We can't afford to let that crop sit. My hybrids—" She dashed a hand across her eyes. Len knew as well as she did that if they bungled the hybrid crop, their credibility with the LSU research center went out the window. LSU wouldn't give a damn why it happened, just that it had.

After she'd said goodbye to Len, she looked at Nick, who'd gotten out of bed and pulled on his pants. For a moment, she couldn't think what to say. What to do. It was an odd feeling for someone accustomed to taking action, a helpless feeling she didn't like at all. "Our harvester is missing," she finally managed to say.

"I heard." He crossed the room, pulled her into his arms. "Do you think it was stolen?" His hand rubbed her back, offering comfort.

She nodded against his shoulder. "Although I can't imagine how they did it. Stealing a harvester isn't exactly as easy as stealing a car. You can't just hot-wire it and drive off. Not without someone noticing."

"What can I do to help?"

"Nothing. I'm sorry, Nick. This wasn't how I'd planned to spend the morning." She stepped out of his arms, even though what she wanted to do was

stand there forever. "I'm going to take a quick shower. My brain's too fuzzy to function. Maybe that will help."

"I'll make coffee."

"You're a lifesaver," she said, and headed for the bathroom.

A short time later, she entered the kitchen and Nick handed her a mug. She sniffed the steaming coffee appreciatively, then sipped. "Oh God, this tastes wonderful. You can actually cook."

"I can make coffee," he said, amused. "And a few other things, but I'm no gourmet cook."

"That's a matter of opinion. Jackson and I can't even boil water," she said, and took another drink. It was hot, strong and heavenly. Exactly what she needed. And so was Nick, she thought, looking at him.

"How sure are you that the harvester is gone?" Nick asked. He'd put his shirt back on, but he was still barefoot, making her think about crawling back in bed with him. But that wasn't going to happen now.

"It's hard to miss. If it were on our property, Len would have found it."

"What will you do if the police don't have any luck turning it up?"

"Try to borrow one. We can do without for a week or so, but much longer and we could be in

real trouble. This couldn't have happened at a worse time. Right now, we run the harvester from daylight to dark.''

''How easy are they to borrow?''

''Let's put it this way, most people don't have an extra one just sitting around.''

''Can you buy a new one?'' He took a sip of his own coffee, then pulled out a chair from the kitchen table and sat.

''Sure.'' She leaned back against the cabinets and looked at him over the rim of her coffee cup. ''For $250,000.''

Nick whistled. ''Expensive suckers, aren't they.''

Casey nodded. ''Very, and this one is brand-new. It's insured, of course, but I don't know how long the money will take to come through.''

''If your insurance company runs true to form, a long time.''

He was right about that, she'd bet. Oh well, if necessary, she'd borrow from the bank. It wasn't as if Bill Harmon, the bank president, didn't know the Fontaines were good for the money. He'd been their banker for as long as Casey could remember. ''I'd better go.'' She topped off her coffee, then hunted for her keys to the truck.

Nick got up and filled his mug, watched as she sifted through the junk on her kitchen counter. ''Ca-

sey." He held up a set of keys. "Is this what you're looking for?"

"Thanks." She took them from him. "I have a bad habit of throwing them anywhere and then not being able to find them."

He smiled. "I noticed that. I have to be at the casino today, and I don't know when I can get away. It opens to the public tonight."

"Oh." She stifled a swift pang of disappointment, surprised at how badly she'd wanted to see him. "Good luck. Or should I say, break a leg?"

"Casey." He set down his mug. "I want to see you tonight. Very much. But it might be late before I can leave."

"That's all right. I have no idea how late I'll be, either. And Nick?" She waited until his eyes met hers and then kissed him. "I want to see you, too."

Maybe the situation wasn't as bad as she'd thought. The police could turn up the machine quickly, or someone might have one to lend them. Yes, she'd overreacted. Everything would turn out fine.

COULD IT BE ANY WORSE? Casey wondered, over an hour later. The police had given the case to Detective Remy Boucherand. Casey had gone to school with Remy and knew he'd do his best to solve the

case, but he didn't try to hide the fact that he didn't hold out much hope for success.

They met in the office, where Casey had been going down her list of friends and neighbors to see who might have a harvester to loan her. She'd covered a third of the list so far, and no one could help. She planned on calling the insurance company as soon as she finished with the police. The company would require proof of her claim, so it had made no sense to notify them before a theft report was filed. After that, she would call Jackson in Mexico. But there was no reason to drag him home when she could handle things.

Remy moved papers off the only other chair in the office and pulled out his notebook. He had the dark, Creole looks so prevalent in the area, but he and Casey had never been more than friends. Last she'd heard, he'd been dating a succession of women, none of whom had managed to get him to the altar.

He took Len through his statement patiently, writing down what Casey already knew. Len had left the machine in the last field he'd harvested, and when he'd returned this morning it was gone. No sign of it anywhere. Not a lot to work with, Casey thought.

Shortly after that, Len and Remy left to look at the scene, and Casey made her calls. Including one

to Aunt Esme to warn her what had happened and that Remy would be questioning her and Tanya. And Nick, she reflected, since he'd been on the property, as well. Of course, she and Nick had been a little too preoccupied to notice much of anything, but she didn't plan to go into detail about that.

As soon as Remy returned, Casey took him up to the big house. "Did you see anything?" she asked as they walked up the dirt road.

Remy nodded. "Trailer tracks. Whoever took the harvester brought one of those big flatbed trailers, loaded it up with—I'd guess—a hydraulic winch and drove off with it. Tell me, Casey, did you hear anything unusual last night? Were you up at the big house?"

"No, I'm living in Wisteria Cottage. But I didn't hear anything." She'd been far too caught up in Nick. "But if you know, or have a good idea, how they stole it, that helps, doesn't it? I mean, it can't be that easy to hide a trailer with a cane harvester sitting on it."

Remy glanced at her, frowning. "I doubt they hid it. If I had to guess, I'd say your harvester is on its way to Mexico by now."

"Mexico? You're kidding."

"Oh, no, *chère*." Remy shook his head. "Not at all. There's a big demand for black-market farm machinery south of the border. We've had cases like

yours in the past. Not a lot of harvesters, but it's not unheard of. If it's like our other cases, they took that trailer right down to the river, loaded the harvester on a barge and sailed it right on out of here. Whole operation took maybe an hour, max.''

Casey's stomach hurt. If the harvester was in Mexico, it didn't seem likely they'd get it back. Which meant she needed to get the insurance company to spring for a replacement. Now.

Esme received them on the back porch, apparently not wanting to taint the tour rooms with police presence. The sound of the workmen, the clattering and banging, could still be heard, though it was muffled. Since she'd moved, Casey had been up to the house often, both to see Megan and to discuss the renovations with Adam. Naturally, she'd seen her aunt, but they hadn't really talked. In fact, Esme seemed determined to act as if her niece didn't exist.

Having known Esme for years, Remy was an expert on handling her. With a wink at Casey, he let her spend a full five minutes inquiring about his family and grilling him on why he hadn't announced his engagement yet. Then he got down to business. He sat at the makeshift breakfast table and pulled out the ubiquitous spiral notebook and pen.

''Has Casey told you about the missing harvester, Miss Esme?''

Esme darted a glance at Casey, then nodded. "She called a short while ago."

"Did you hear anything unusual last night? Or see anything out of the ordinary? Len said he left the harvester around eight-thirty, so it would be sometime after that."

"No. It's difficult to hear anything from the fields. And I don't make a habit of peering out the windows late at night."

"Is the nanny here? I'd like to talk to her, as well."

"I'll send her down. She went out but returned around ten. You might ask Cassandra." Esme flicked a reproving glance at her. "No doubt she was out until all hours, gambling and such. Though, of course, since she saw fit to move out, I'm sure I couldn't say."

Well, she had just said it, hadn't she? Casey thought irritably.

Remy turned to her and lifted an eyebrow. "Casey? Do you have anything to add?"

Casey gritted her teeth. "I was out late. I went to the opening of the White Gold casino. Nick brought me back, but neither of us heard or saw anything unusual. I'd have told you if I had."

"She's talking about that gambler," Esme interjected. "Nick Devlin, the one my nephew has decided to install in the *garçonnière.*"

"Nick's an old friend of Jackson's," Casey explained. "He's managing the White Gold until the new owner takes over. I'm sure you can find him there, but I doubt he heard anything, either. He would have said something."

Esme sniffed but didn't comment.

"All the same," Remy said, "it won't hurt to talk to him. I'd like to speak to whoever was on the grounds last night." He turned to Esme and gave her his most charming smile. "Could I ask you to get the nanny?"

After she left, Remy sent a speculative look at Casey. "Might just be my nasty, suspicious nature, but I sense a little tension between you and your auntie."

Casey crossed her legs and swung one foot. "You'd have to be deaf, dumb and blind not to. We don't see eye to eye about…certain things."

"And would one of those certain things happen to be this gambler? Nick Devlin, I think your auntie said his name was."

Frowning, she started to deny it, then shrugged. "Is it that obvious?"

"I've known you a long time, *chère*," he reminded her. *"Oui."*

"Why so interested, Remy? None of this has anything to do with the missing harvester."

"A good detective likes to get the full picture," he said virtuously.

"Ditto a nosy detective."

"Ah, now you've hurt my feelings." He put a hand over his heart.

"Impossible. You don't have any."

Remy laughed, as Esme returned with Tanya. "Cassandra, I'd like to speak to you," she said in her most commanding voice.

"I was about to go to Duke's office and contact the insurance company," Casey said, rising. "I don't have time right now, Aunt Esme."

"I suggest you make time," her aunt said, and turned on her heel.

"Good luck," Remy murmured. "From the looks of Miss Esme, you're going to need it. I'll be in touch about the case," he added, and picked up his notebook again.

Casey wasn't normally a woman who shied from confrontation. She only wished she weren't having this one when she was so short on sleep and patience.

CHAPTER ELEVEN

ESME WAS WAITING FOR HER in Duke's office. That alone indicated she was upset, since Esme didn't ordinarily venture in there. She considered it Duke's domain, and the rest of the house, hers.

Angelique had always relied heavily on Esme in the running of the house, but to be fair, Esme had never challenged Angelique after she'd put her foot down. Which was the only reason Esme tolerated having Betty around. As a shirttail relation of Angelique's, Betty would stay until Angelique fired her, which she never would.

But for now it was just Casey and her aunt. And Casey was in no mood to listen to Esme's numerous complaints. She had more important things on her mind.

Duke's office had been one of Casey's favorite rooms from childhood. It was tucked away at the back of the house on the ground floor, overlooking the side yard. The wallpaper was a dark, masculine brocade. Paintings hung from the high ceilings on wires that were screwed into the wide cornice en-

circling the room. Two green leather armchairs faced the desk, and a very uncomfortable green leather couch studded with brass buttons sat against one wall. A Waterford crystal decanter full of whiskey and four matching glasses graced a side table.

Duke's desk, an antique cherry wood with hidden drawers, dominated the room. Matching file cabinets occupied the wall behind it. Story was, the desk had belonged to John "Duke" Wayne once upon a time, and so naturally, Duke Fontaine had to have it. Casey had many memories of the Duke, seated in the enormous leather desk chair, puffing on his pipe from time to time, and holding court over a variety of businessmen. It was a powerful room, furnished with a powerful man in mind.

Today, however, Casey held the power. She walked in, bypassed her aunt on the couch—Toodles lying across her feet—and sat in her father's chair. Lacing her fingers together and placing her hands on the desk blotter, Casey said, "I have several calls to make, Aunt Esme, so let's make this quick."

"I certainly hope one of those calls is to your brother. Or have you called him already? When is he coming home?"

Casey silently counted to ten. "I haven't called Jackson yet. I'm planning to as soon as I have something more definite to tell him."

Esme looked astonished. "But we need him here.

Surely you don't expect to handle this situation yourself. With Duke gone—''

"With Duke and Jackson gone, I'm in charge. Of everything," she added. "There's no reason to force Jackson to come home early from his meeting. Not when I'm perfectly capable of taking care of things.''

"You'll do as you please, I'm sure, just as you always do. Just as you're doing with that man Jackson dragged home. You don't care how disgraceful your behavior is—''

"Aunt Esme," Casey interrupted wearily, "can we postpone this discussion of my shortcomings until later? Is there anything you *really* need to talk to me about? Or did you only drag me in here to complain?''

Esme rose, dumping Toodles off her feet unceremoniously. The little dog barked and wagged his tail, then ran to the door, clearly wondering what was keeping his mistress. "Yes, there is. I want to know more about this Adam Ross. What do you know about him? Anything that didn't come from Nick Devlin?''

Casey pulled the rein on her temper a little tighter. It wasn't unreasonable for Esme to question Adam's credentials, but her timing sucked. "I thought you liked Adam.''

''Whether I like him or not has no bearing on the matter,'' Esme said primly.

Casey sighed. ''I checked him out fully before I hired him. He has several excellent references, including one from the Marchands,'' she added, naming a family Esme had known for decades. ''If you're worried, call Christina Marchand. I'm sure she'd love to gossip with you about any number of things, including Adam Ross. If that's all, I really have to call the insurance company now.''

Esme stalked out, heels ringing on the wooden floor, Toodles yapping ecstatically behind her. Casey put her head in her hands. She hated being on the outs with Esme. She loved her aunt, even if they never agreed on anything. But Casey didn't have the time or desire to tiptoe around the woman right now.

She got up and went to the file cabinet, where she flipped through folders until she found the one labeled ''Insurance.''

By the time she ended the call with the insurance company a nagging headache had developed into a raging migraine. The claims agent had been kind and sympathetic, and had promised help as soon as was humanly possible, but help still wouldn't be coming any too soon. Claims took a lot of time to process, and that was that.

While she was putting the file back, she ran across the old plans for the fountain Angelique had had

built, shortly after she and Duke were married. It was the custom for every generation of Fontaines to add a new fountain, which was why so many would be found on the estate. Casey and Jackson hadn't gotten around to planning their fountain yet. Casey put the plans away with a sigh. Building a new fountain had just slid even farther down the list of things to do.

Casey left a voice mail in Jackson's hotel room asking him to call her as soon as he got the message. Then she headed out to see Bill Harmon. The banker had known her since she was a child. He wouldn't mind her barging into his house on a Saturday, as long as it was important.

"SORRY TO BOTHER YOU on a weekend," Casey told Bill Harmon as she preceded him into his study. "But I wouldn't be here if it weren't important."

"No, no, quite all right," the banker said, motioning for her to sit as he seated himself behind his big, mahogany desk. He was in his late fifties with green eyes, gray hair and a permanent tan from golfing. "How are the travelers? Have you heard from them lately?"

"No. I think my mother put her foot down. She knows that given half a chance, Duke would spend all his time on the phone discussing business."

Harmon laughed. "True, true. So tell me, Casey, what can I do for you?"

"I need a loan. Just a temporary one," she added hastily when he frowned.

"What's the problem? The fire?"

"No, we've been able to cover those expenses until the insurance comes through, but now we've had another disaster. And this one is even worse. Someone stole the cane harvester."

"Stole your harvester?" he repeated. "That machine is huge. How is that possible?"

Casey shook her head. "I don't know. It disappeared sometime last night. And since we haven't seen any money from the fire, I don't expect the new claim will come through soon." Her fingers tightened on the arms of the chair. "That's the problem— I've got to get another harvester now. The John Deere Company holds the first loan, and they won't give us another. Not until things are sorted out. As it is, it's going to take a few days before another machine is available. If we go too long without one, we run the risk of losing the entire harvest. Or most of it, anyway."

Harmon rubbed his jaw, frowning. "You can't borrow one?"

"No. I've tried." He looked less than thrilled, she thought, wondering why it was such a big deal. "I'll

pay back the loan as soon as the insurance money comes in, of course.''

''Refresh my memory. What does a harvester run nowadays?''

''About $250,000. I'd like to finance this one through the bank, since the dealer is already unhappy about the stolen one.'' He was still frowning, saying nothing. ''Bill, I wouldn't be here if I weren't desperate.'' God, she hated to beg, but she had no choice. Why was he being so difficult? ''You know the Fontaines are good for it. Unless...'' She hesitated, then asked, ''Is there a problem I need to be aware of?''

Bill hemmed and hawed, but he didn't answer her question. ''Casey, there's really nothing I can do from home. I can look into it Monday morning and give you a call.''

Frustrated, Casey stood. ''Fine. I'll talk to you Monday, then. Sorry to bother you.'' In the meantime, she needed to call Suttler's, the local John Deere store, and have them locate a new harvester as soon as possible. She didn't think there would be a problem, but then, she hadn't thought there would be a problem with the bank, either.

She listened with half an ear as Bill went with her to the door, anxious to call Jackson to see if he had any clue what was going on. Obviously, he hadn't gotten the message yet or he would have

phoned her. She winced, thinking it would be a double whammy for her brother, telling him about the missing harvester as well as something odd going on with the bank.

Too impatient to wait, she dialed Aunt Esme and got Jackson's number at the hotel the minute she got in the car. By some minor miracle, she caught him in his room.

"I was just about to call you," he said.

"Thank God you're there," she said without preamble.

"What's wrong? It's not Megan, is it? I talked to her last night and she sounded all right."

"Megan's fine. The harvester's been stolen." She gave him a brief rundown of what had happened, including the insurance company dragging their feet and the fact that Remy thought it unlikely they'd get the machine back. "So I went to Bill Harmon, thinking I could get an interim loan for a new one."

"Good thinking. Listen, Casey, I can check the flights and possibly be back tonight."

"No. Absolutely not. I can handle this, Jackson."

"I know you can. But you shouldn't have to deal with the problem alone."

"You'll be home in a few days, anyway. Don't reschedule. But that's not what I wanted to talk to you about. It's Bill Harmon. He acted very strange when I asked him for the loan."

"What do you mean?"

"I mean, he put me off until Monday and acted like he didn't want to do it. Are we having financial problems I don't know about?" That would be the icing on the cake. And knowing Duke, her brother probably wasn't much better informed than she was.

"Of course not." Jackson sounded impatient. "At least, I don't think so. But you know how close-mouthed Duke is. He wasn't exactly forthcoming about business before he left town. Maybe he's taken out a loan we don't know about. Did Bill say anything specific, or was it just a feeling you got?"

"More of a feeling, I guess." But it sure had been a strong one. "Jackson, I'm worried. I'm afraid the insurance company is going to take forever to reimburse us. If the bank won't come through…" Her voice trailed off.

Jackson was silent, too, probably thinking about how it would affect them if they couldn't get a harvester.

As she pulled into the gravel drive in front of her house, she renewed her determination. She did not intend to lose this crop. No matter what she had to do, she'd get another harvester.

"Have you told Duke?" Jackson finally said.

"No. He can't do anything from three thousand miles away. Why bother him and Maman?" Besides, she wasn't about to admit to her father that

she couldn't handle the business. "And if we tell him about the harvester, we're going to have to tell him about the fire, too."

"Good point." He sighed again, and Casey pictured him rubbing the bridge of his nose, the way he did when he was worried. "I'm due back next Thursday. I want you to promise to let me know if you need me there earlier. And call me Monday once you hear from Bill. They're not the only bank. We can approach someone else if necessary."

"True," Casey said, brightening a bit. "I hadn't considered that, since we always deal with Harmon. Look, I'm at the cottage now and I want to call Suttler's and see if they have a cane harvester readily available."

"Good luck with that," Jackson said wryly. "You know they're hard to come by, especially now."

"I know. But maybe we'll get lucky for a change. I'll be in touch."

As she hung up, her natural optimism began to reassert itself. Despite whatever odd things were going on with Harmon, surely he'd give them the loan. And once she was able to bring in the harvest, their lives would get back to normal.

CHAPTER TWELVE

NICK DIDN'T MAKE IT to Casey's place until after midnight. Since it was so late, he considered not going in, but when he saw her lights on, he couldn't resist.

The public opening of the casino had taken a lot of his attention, but not so much that he didn't think about Casey. A lot. More than he normally thought about a woman.

It was a strange experience for him to be so wrapped up in a woman. He wasn't sure he liked it. But he didn't seem to have a choice. At the casino a show-stopper blonde had made it clear she was interested in taking him home with her. He'd turned her down, which wasn't unusual since he was involved with someone. But his total lack of interest in the woman had been very far from the norm. He wanted to see Casey, period.

"You look tired," he said after he kissed her hello. His fault, since he'd kept her up most of the night making love. But he didn't regret that and didn't believe she did, either.

She led him to the couch, shooting him a wry grin over her shoulder. "I am tired. But I'm more worried than anything else."

"Can I do something to help?"

She shook her head. "Not unless you want to loan me $250,000 for a new cane harvester. I'm afraid the bank's going to turn us down."

He didn't think she'd been serious, but he offered, anyway. "Okay. When do you need it?"

Her jaw dropped. "Are you crazy? I was kidding. Besides, you can't offer to loan me that kind of money. You hardly know me."

Nick cupped her chin and smiled at her, then dropped a kiss on her lips. "I know you. You'd never renege on a loan. And it's just for a few weeks, isn't it?"

She covered his hand with hers, her eyes jade green with emotion. "Nick, I can't take the money from you. It's sweet of you to offer, but I can't. Jackson would have a stroke, too."

"It's an offer to help out a friend. Why can't you accept it?"

She didn't answer, just frowned at him, so he added, "I'll have a contract drawn up. We can make it as official as you want."

"It won't work."

"Why not?"

"Because." She leaned forward and kissed him.

"You're a little more than a friend. It wouldn't be right." She settled back into the couch. "I'm sure I'm overreacting, anyway. The banker's supposed to call me Monday and let me know."

"Will you tell me if he says no?"

She nodded. "I'll be so mad I won't be able to keep my mouth shut, I'm sure. But that doesn't mean I'm taking your money."

He smiled. They'd see about that. He put his arm around her and pulled her close against his side. Her hand came up to rest over his heart.

"Did Remy get a chance to talk to you? About last night?" she asked.

It took him a moment to remember who she was talking about. "The detective? Yeah, he did. I don't think I was much help, since I didn't see or hear a thing." He'd been far too busy with Casey. "But he does agree with me that you need to be careful."

Casey frowned and pulled back to look at him. "Be careful? About what?"

"Casey, hasn't it occurred to you that someone might have it in for you? Or your family, anyway."

"Have it in for us?" She looked at him blankly. "You mean, because of the fire?"

He nodded. "They think that fire was arson, remember? It was only luck that you got in the kitchen in time to drag your aunt out. Then, a couple of

weeks later, your harvester disappears. Sounds too convenient to be coincidence.''

She rubbed her temples. ''I've been so focused on getting a new harvester, I haven't had time to think about it. But it does seem odd, doesn't it?''

''Yes, it does. Your father's a powerful man, from what I hear. Powerful men tend to make powerful enemies.'' He waited for her to answer, and when she only frowned, he continued. ''Or it could be an enemy of yours.''

She laughed. ''I don't have any enemies. At least, not that I know of.''

''Everyone has enemies,'' he said. ''What about that man we saw the other day?''

''What man?''

''The employee you fired. He was anything but friendly.''

She looked confused, then her brow cleared. ''Harold Broderick, you mean? The one I let go for drinking on the job?'' She shook her head. ''He's harmless. Most of the time he's too drunk to do anything useful.''

He hadn't seemed harmless to Nick. He'd seemed like just the type of man to take his anger out on a woman. ''Still, it's something to think about. And you should tell the police about him. If only to be safe.''

Casey continued to look skeptical. ''You're really

reaching. I can see Duke as a possible target. He's not the easiest person in the world to get along with. And I'm sure he's made enemies in the business. But me?" She shook her head, still smiling. "That's pretty far-fetched."

"Is it?" He waited a moment, until her eyes met his, and asked, "What about Murray?"

Her mouth tightened as she looked at him. "Murray's a friend of mine."

"A friend who wants to be more," he reminded her. "From what you said, he wasn't happy when you turned him down."

She got up and paced away a few steps, then turned to face him. "I can't believe Murray would stoop so low. Besides, this all began with the fire, and Murray hadn't told me about his feelings then. If you're determined to give him jealousy as a motive, that doesn't work."

Nick shrugged. "I'm not determined to give him anything. I'm simply saying you should consider it. Murray got to Bellefontaine pretty quickly after the fire started. Did you call him?"

"No. Tanya was supposed to but she didn't. He said…" She hesitated, then finished, "He said he and his father had seen the smoke, or the flames or something."

"Maybe they saw them because they were watch-

ing for them. Roland Dewalt made his feelings about you clear last night.''

''Oh, come on, Nick. Because two men have said ugly things to me, you figure they're out to get me?'' Casey scrubbed her hands over her face. ''I think you're off-base. Granted, Roland is a jerk, but I don't see him as the mastermind behind all this. And I sure can't believe it of Murray. Whatever else, he's always been a good friend to me.''

''He doesn't want to be your friend, remember? He wants to be your lover. Hell, he wants to marry you, doesn't he?''

She gave a jerky nod.

''So he wants to marry you, and not only did you shoot him down, you took up with another man.''

She frowned at him again. ''That doesn't mean he's been sneaking around starting fires and stealing farm machinery.'' She shook her head. ''Sorry, I just don't believe it.''

Nick didn't care for the pull of jealousy her defense of Murray caused him. He hadn't forgotten that Murray would be around, waiting to try his luck with Casey the minute Nick left town. Unless he didn't leave town.

But what would he do in Baton Rouge? With the exception of his college years, he'd never stayed in one place longer than a few months. He didn't think

he was capable of sticking around. Even if Casey did make the idea very tempting.

"Nick, is something wrong? Why are you looking at me so strangely?"

Possibly because he'd just figured out he was falling in love with her. But it was such an alien concept to him that he wasn't about to tell her. "I was wondering why we were talking about Murray when I can think of much more pleasant things to do."

She gave him a slow smile, walked over and held out a hand. "I didn't mean to bore you with all my problems."

"You didn't bore me." He took her hand and pulled her onto his lap. "You could never bore me."

She laughed and wrapped her arms around his neck. "Of course I could. Let me start talking about sugarcane hybrids, and I guarantee your eyes will glaze over."

"I'm not worried." He kissed her forehead. "But you are." And it surprised him how badly he wanted to take that worry away for her.

She smiled, a little ruefully. "The problem is the timing. Harvesters don't simply appear by magic. They're hard to come by. Even if everything goes well, we probably won't have the machine for a week. That's a lot of time to miss."

"Is there no other way to harvest? Didn't they use to harvest by hand?"

"Yes, with machetes. But we went mechanical years ago. All our laborers have gone to other jobs. Besides, it's brutal. I'm not sure we'd find anyone willing, at least no one who's not an illegal alien. None of the migrant workers would touch it." She sighed and leaned her head against his shoulder. "Thanks."

"For what? I haven't done anything."

"Yes, you did. You listened to me. And gave me a shoulder to lean on."

"Anytime." He took her face in his hands and kissed her, felt her mouth soften, give in to his.

She drew back and looked at him, her eyes big, green, luminous. And questioning.

"Casey? What is it?"

"Nothing. Make love to me, Nick."

BY THE TIME Jackson came home Thursday evening, things weren't much better at Bellefontaine. Casey had gone to Duke's office to wait for her brother for a number of reasons, the main one being to get away from Esme. Jackson had gone up to tuck Megan in, promising to join Casey after he read his daughter a story.

Bill Harmon had agreed to give them the interim loan, though he wouldn't tell her why he'd been skittish in the first place. Casey had thought about pressing him on it, but decided she'd leave that up

to Jackson. She had more urgent concerns, such as wondering when the replacement harvester would come in.

And worrying that she'd fallen head-over-heels in love with Nick Devlin. She'd lectured herself a dozen times, but it didn't matter. She'd fallen in love and there was nothing she could do to change that fact.

As for Nick, she couldn't be sure what he thought. She knew he cared about her, but he'd said nothing about remaining in Baton Rouge once his commitment to the White Gold ended. She hadn't asked him, either. Maybe she didn't want to know his answer.

Jackson came in, interrupting her thoughts. Her heart sank as she saw her aunt hard on his heels with Toodles bringing up the rear. Just what she didn't need—another confrontation with Esme.

Esme was in full swing, too, railing at Jackson. "If you don't care that your sister is making a spectacle of herself, I do. I have more respect for the family name—"

Jackson held up a hand. "Aunt Esme, I'm sorry, but I can't see Casey doing anything to disgrace the family name. What's she done that's so terrible?"

"Done?" Esme stared at him, her body quivering with outrage. "*Mon Dieu,* she's been practically living in sin with that gambler. I'm sure tongues are

wagging all over Baton Rouge. When I think of what your parents will say, I positively shudder."

Jackson looked at his sister, a frown gathering. "I didn't realize you and Nick had—" he glanced at Esme and continued "—grown that close."

Casey rose, holding onto her temper. She was used to her family butting in, and generally tolerated it. But today they were getting on her last nerve. "Well, we have. Not that it's your, or Aunt Esme's, or anybody else's damn business. I'm a grown woman, for heaven's sake. This is ridiculous." She put a hand on Jackson's arm. "Talk to her, Jackson. Aunt Esme has taken a totally unreasonable dislike to Nick, and I'm sick and tired of it."

He looked at her for a moment as if unsure what to say, then he smiled. He took Aunt Esme by the arm and began walking to the door with her. "Aunt Esme, Casey and I need to discuss business now. I'll talk with you tomorrow, all right?"

Esme jerked her arm away and marched out the office door, not quite slamming it behind her.

Casey rolled her eyes. "Thanks, Jackson. I don't think I could have stood another minute of Aunt Esme's histrionics."

"She loves you. She's worried about you." He paused, then added, "So am I."

"Thanks, but you don't need to be. I'm perfectly capable of running my own affairs."

"Agreed. But you can't expect me not to worry."

"You're not going to start saying ugly things about Nick, are you? Because I'll warn you right now—"

"How serious are you about this relationship?"

Casey moved away to stare out the window at one of the lighted fountains. Maybe she should talk to her brother. She needed someone to talk to, and Viv had been scarce lately—not that Casey blamed her. Viv hadn't been married long, so it was only natural she'd be caught up in her new husband and life. But Casey still missed her.

"I don't know. If you're asking if I'm in love with him…"

"Are you?"

Casey turned to look at him. "Yes. And no, he doesn't know. So I'd prefer that little fact stayed between us."

Jackson sighed and tugged on his hair. "You never do anything the easy way, do you? Nick's not…he's not an easy man to know. We met several years ago, but he's never been very talkative about his past. And he's never stayed in one place for long."

"He's an orphan," Casey said. "I get the feeling that has something to do with him not putting down roots."

"Interesting," Jackson said. "You already know

more about him than I did. Maybe there is hope for you two.''

''I guess we'll find out, won't we? In the meantime,'' she said, walking over to one of the chairs and sitting, ''we need to talk business. How much do you know about our family's financial situation?''

Jackson sat in one of the other chairs. ''Less than I'd like to. Prying information out of Duke is always a challenge.''

Casey frowned and linked her hands around her knee. ''I think you should talk to Bill Harmon. He won't discuss anything with me. Maybe you'll have better luck.''

''I can try. When do you expect the new harvester to come in?''

''I'm praying it's in by early next week. If we have to go on much longer without one, our losses are going to be heavy.'' In terms of both the harvest and their relationship with LSU. But she didn't need to elaborate on that with her brother. He understood the sugar business.

Jackson sighed and squeezed the bridge of his nose. ''Guess there's nothing to do other than hope we get lucky for a change. Do you want me to call the insurance company again? See if I can get them to move more quickly?''

''Sure. Remy doesn't have any leads. At least, he

didn't last time I talked to him, which was this afternoon.''

"I'll call him and the insurance company tomorrow, and then drop by the bank." He gave Casey a searching look. "You've got enough on your plate," he said, and went out.

Casey wished she could believe he'd been referring to the harvest, but she had a sinking feeling he was talking about Nick. It had been a long time since she'd trusted a man with her heart—and look what had happened then. Could she be making just as big a mistake this time?

CHAPTER THIRTEEN

NICK KNEW JACKSON had been out of town for a few weeks, so when he answered a page to come to the main level entrance, his old friend was the last person he'd expected to see.

"When did you get back?" Nick asked him, shaking hands and wondering what the other man wanted. He couldn't tell much from Jackson's expression, but then, Jackson Fontaine had always had an exceptional poker face. Nick had discovered that early on, when Jackson had sat in on a card game with him and cleaned everyone out, including Nick.

Jackson looked around at the game room. "A few hours ago. Looks good, Nick. Heard the opening was a success. Sorry I missed it."

"It went well, but I'm sure you didn't come down here your first night home just to shoot the breeze."

Jackson dragged his attention away from a very pretty brunette who had waved at him, and smiled at Nick. "No, you're right about that. Can we go someplace and talk?"

"Sure." Nick led the way to his office, then

closed the door behind them. "You've talked to Casey, haven't you?"

"I've talked to Casey daily since the harvester was stolen. But, yes, I've seen her tonight." He paused, stroked a hand over his jaw. "I talked to Aunt Esme, too. Tell me, Nick, how did you manage to get so high on Esme's shit list so quickly?"

So, Jackson didn't intend to circle around any issues. Good. "Could be the fact that I'm dating your sister. Your aunt has a major problem with that. Are you here to tell me you do, too?"

"From what I hear it's a little more than dating." He held up a hand before Nick could speak. "But that's not my business, or Esme's." He paused before saying, "Casey's a grown woman and she's certainly capable of picking her...friends without my interference. I have to tell you, though—" he leaned forward and caught Nick's gaze "—if you hurt her, you're toast. *Comprends?*"

"I understand, don't worry. I don't have any plans to hurt Casey."

Jackson sat back in his chair, making himself comfortable. "Sometimes things happen that we don't plan."

They sure as hell did. Like falling in love for the first time. And knowing it was futile. "What do you want me to say? I care about Casey. She's not like anyone I've ever met." Not like anyone he ever

would meet, he suspected. "If you're asking my intentions, I can tell you right now, they don't include marriage."

Jackson frowned. "I had a feeling that's where you stood. Does Casey know this?"

He shrugged. "She knows." They'd never planned on anything more than a short-term romance. But he knew it had become more than that. For both of them.

"Are you sure about that?" Jackson's gaze met Nick's, his eyes dark blue and eminently readable. If Nick didn't do the right thing, Jackson was ready to take him apart.

"I'm sure. Why, did she say something to you?"

Jackson hesitated, then shook his head.

"Then, why are you so sure that Casey wants something serious?"

He looked troubled. "Because I know her. She might not say anything to you, but she damn sure feels it."

Nick got up and paced the room, wishing he knew how to explain his feelings. Wishing he even understood his feelings. But why would he? Until he'd met Casey, he'd never *had* these feelings for a woman.

He stopped at the window, looked out at the lights playing over the water. "Damn it, Jackson, this isn't just some casual fling to me. I care about Casey."

He loved her, not that it mattered. Loving Casey didn't mean the past thirty-six years of his life would disappear and not leave their mark on him.

"You care about her, but not enough to marry her."

"No." He turned to face Jackson. "I care about her too much to marry her. It wouldn't work. Better she find that out now than later."

Unsmiling, Jackson got up. "I can almost believe you mean that. Almost," he added, and walked out the door.

Nick cursed softly as the door closed behind his friend. He didn't blame Jackson for being angry at him. Or for wanting to protect his sister. Hell, that's what families were supposed to do, wasn't it? Just because Nick had never had a family didn't mean he didn't know that.

He knew he should talk to Casey. Knew he needed to make sure she understood that even though their feelings had changed, nothing else had. He still couldn't stay with her, no matter how much he might want to. Because in the end, he would only hurt her.

But once he talked to her, once they brought everything into the open, he would lose her. And he couldn't face that. Not yet.

IT WAS LATE, but Casey couldn't think about sleep, or relaxing, either. Her life was spiraling out of con-

trol. The cane was in jeopardy because someone had stolen their harvester. Someone who might or might not be their enemy. Her love life, which up until recently had been nonexistent, was now a hotbed of activity. That was unsettling in itself, but the situation was made worse by the fact that she'd fallen for a man who'd said from the first that he'd be leaving.

She was at odds with her family, too. Or at least with Esme. In the week since Jackson had come back, Esme still hadn't forgiven Casey. And though she and Esme had always had their differences, Casey had never doubted her aunt's love. Until recently.

Earlier, Casey had been in her office, trying to catch up with paperwork, until she'd finally gotten so sick of it she'd come home. But every time she closed her eyes she worried again. Thanks to Jackson sweet-talking Harmon, they got the loan. The replacement harvester had finally arrived; but had it come in time to save them from disaster? She couldn't say, and neither could Len. They wouldn't have to write off the entire harvest, but they'd lost a good portion of the crop.

She'd even begun composing a letter to the LSU agricultural department in case the hybrid crop didn't produce as expected.

Realizing lying in bed was useless, Casey got up and went back to the greenhouse, hoping boring paperwork would send her to sleep when nothing else had.

As she approached the office, she heard a *thud* inside. Pausing with her hand on the door knob, she heard it again. She opened the door, stopping dead on the threshold. Casey didn't know who was more surprised, she or the big, beefy man who stood over the CPU unit with a crowbar.

Harold Broderick?

Broderick glanced up at her, then brought the iron bar crashing down on the unit.

"Stop!" Casey shouted, springing forward. "The police are on their way!" A lie, but he didn't have to know that. "Stop it, right now!"

He paid no attention to her, but gave the poor, battered unit a couple more hefty strokes. He turned to the monitor just before she reached him. The glass screen exploded, but luckily for Casey, Broderick took the brunt of the flying shards. She grabbed his arm as he swung it back.

He snarled and backhanded her, then continued to beat on the machine. Casey reeled away, dazed by the blow. Shaking her head to clear it, Casey grabbed him again, this time managing to bang his arm down on the corner of the desk. He cursed and the bar fell clattering to the floor.

Deprived of his tool, he grabbed her around the throat before she could move away. "Bitch," he growled as he squeezed. "Think you can get rid of me? I'll show you."

The sickly smell of whiskey washed over her, triggering a memory she'd pushed out of her mind. Memories of the day she'd fired Broderick and he'd towered over her, screaming incoherent threats. She'd been uneasy then, but not afraid, knowing Len was close by if she needed him. Tonight, she was on her own.

Casey clawed at Broderick's hands, then, realizing that was futile, she tried to jab his eyes with her thumbs. He gave an enraged roar and choked her harder. She'd thought him malicious, though essentially harmless, all bluster and vague threats that he'd had no intention of carrying out. But the hands tightening around her neck felt anything but harmless.

She was an idiot. She should have run for help when she'd first seen him, but she'd acted on instinct, instead. Casey didn't back down from a fight, she confronted it. In this case, stupidly. Maybe even fatally.

Her vision grayed. Above the blood pounding in her ears she heard a shout. For an instant, Broderick's hands loosened and she jerked back enough to bring her knee straight up into his groin. He howled

in pain, but didn't let go. She raised her knee again, but missed him. Then, suddenly, she was free.

Clutching at her throat, she gasped for air. Two men struggled, crashing to the floor seconds later. Nick, she thought, barely recognizing him for the fury of his expression. He and Broderick rolled over and over, oblivious to the glass on the floor, crashing into the desk, the computer unit, the chair, the wall. In the confined space between her desk and the back wall, the men didn't have much room to maneuver, and the sounds they made—flesh striking flesh, curses and grunts—echoed in the silence.

Her breath returned, but when she attempted to speak, to shout, her voice emerged in a croak. Undecided, she tried to think of what she could do to help. She thought about the phone, but the two men were between her and the desk. Her gaze lit on the crowbar and she took a couple of hasty steps toward it.

The men were also between her and the weapon, with Nick on top. He pulled back his arm, ready to land a blow on the other man's face, when Broderick grabbed the crowbar, raised it and slammed it down across Nick's shoulder.

Casey heard it, a sickening *thunk* of metal striking flesh and then a shout of pain. She gave an outraged cry and sprang toward them, but they crashed into her and she fell, going down in a tangle of men,

sweat and blood. They moved away from her, but she saw Broderick lift the crowbar again and hit Nick with it, this time across the ribs. By the time she scrambled to her knees, Broderick had thrown Nick aside and run out the door.

"Son of a bitch!" Nick said, and got up, clutching his side and grimacing, obviously in pain. He took a few steps toward the door, then stopped and looked back at Casey. "Are you all right?"

Still unable to speak, she nodded. He headed outside, but came back moments later. Casey was still standing behind the desk, staring at the wreck the man had made of her office and computer.

"He's disappeared into the fields. There's no way I can find him in this darkness. Goddamn it, if I could have gotten my hands on him again, I'd have—" He broke off when Casey ran to him, and he gathered her in his arms.

"I know who he is," she said, her voice muffled against his shoulder and hoarse still.

"I recognized him, too. It was Broderick, wasn't it?" She started to speak, but he hushed her. "Don't try to talk. I'm calling 9-1-1." His arms tightened, and she could hardly breathe, but he felt so strong, so comforting, she didn't care. She clung to him as if he were a life raft in a raging sea.

Finally he pulled back to look at her. "Are you really all right? Just nod."

Casey nodded, feeling tears spring to her eyes. "What about you?" she managed to say. "He hurt you." She touched his side where Broderick had hit him with the crowbar.

Nick sucked in a breath, then gently removed her hand. "Nothing but bruises."

"And these," she said, running a hand along his arm. The skin was abraded with glass shards. Not life-threatening, but surely painful.

"No big deal. Not like this." His fingers touched her throat, so gently she might have imagined it. "Damn Broderick," he murmured. "He'd better pray the police get to him before I do."

Their eyes met, and Casey sucked in a breath. She'd never seen that particular look in Nick's eyes. Never really imagined she would. But it was there, as clear and shiny and true as anything she'd ever seen. He loved her. Even if he hadn't said it, Casey was never more sure of anything in her life. Nick loved her.

"COME ON, *chère*," Remy Boucherand said a short while later, "you have to go to the hospital. As soon as you give your statement. I wouldn't be doing my job if I didn't insist on it." He looked at Nick. "You talk to her. Maybe she'll listen to you."

They had moved into the greenhouse itself, where there were benches to sit on while they gave the

detective their statements. Nick's shoulder and ribs hurt like hell, but worse was the fear that lingered after seeing that bastard with his hands around Casey's throat.

"He's right," Nick said. "You have to let the doctor check you out. Quit being stubborn about it."

She turned to him. "I'll go if you will."

Nick started to protest, but Casey ignored him, telling Remy, "He was hit with a crowbar. Twice. At least. Tell him he has to go, too."

Nick gave in. If it would get Casey to go, he didn't mind. Much. "All right. It's a deal. So, how about we give our statements and then go to the hospital and get it over with?"

Boucherand pulled out his notebook and jotted a few notes. "Good deal. Now, Casey, you arrived first?" She nodded. "Tell me what happened."

"I'll give you the details, but the first thing I should tell you is that Nick and I both recognized him."

Remy's eyes sharpened, as did his voice. "Go on."

"Harold Broderick. He is—was—an employee of mine. I had to fire him earlier this year. He ran some of the tractors, and we'd been thinking about letting him run the harvester when Len couldn't, but he didn't work out."

"Why not?" the detective asked.

Her hands shook a little and she clasped them together. "He came to work drunk. I gave him a warning the first time and sent him home. But the second time, he was gone. I can't afford to have men operating our machinery drunk."

Remy nodded, taking more notes. "Did he have a problem with that?"

Casey frowned and her hand crept up to her throat. "He made a bunch of threats, but I figured it was the liquor talking. It was nothing very substantial, just 'you'll be sorry, bitch' kind of statements." She shrugged. "I never imagined he was serious. I guess I was wrong."

"Looks like," Remy agreed. "Anything else? When did you fire him?"

Casey rubbed a hand over her brow. "I can't remember exactly. I could look it up." She stopped and shook her head. "Well, I could if I had a working computer."

"Don't you have backup disks?"

"Sure, of the most important stuff. I don't know if the employee records are backed up, though. Probably not, but I can look."

Remy nodded. "If not, I'm sure there's another way we can find out. Was this recent, though?" He looked at her searchingly. "Say, before the fire at Bellefontaine?"

She let out a breath as if she'd been holding it.

"Oh, my God. It was about a week or two before that."

"I think I'm beginning to see a pattern," Remy said.

Nick had already gotten a good impression of Boucherand from meeting with him about the stolen harvester, but his opinion rose another notch. The detective appeared to be both thorough and insightful.

"Add this to it," Nick said. "Casey and I saw him the day before the casino opening. We were having lunch at Brew-Bachers and he was there. I should have pounded the scum then," he said, his mouth tightening with anger.

Casey put her hand on his thigh and patted it. "Nick didn't like the way he acted."

"What did he do?"

"Same thing as before. He said a lot of ugly things." She paused. "I figured he was drunk again and blew him off."

"And I let him go," Nick said. "I didn't do a damn thing to the bastard. I should have broken his face." But Casey had asked him not to, so he'd given in to her.

"You did the right thing, Nick," Casey said. "The man was drunk, and besides, he left the restaurant when he saw the manager coming over. There wasn't any reason to cause a scene."

Nick's eyes met the detective's. "I should have taken care of him then. Casey wouldn't be sitting here with bruises on her throat if I had." He clenched his fist, then loosened it. It was swollen from his earlier encounter with Broderick and hurt like hell.

"Don't beat yourself up over it," Remy advised. "Doesn't sound like anyone thought he was dangerous before this. Besides—" a grin widened his mouth "—if you'd busted his face in a public place, I'd have had to haul you in, and then Casey would be on my back."

"It would have been worth it," Nick said. He looked at Casey, thinking the bruises had darkened in the short period of time they'd been talking. "If it would have stopped him from putting his hands on Casey."

He didn't want any man's hands on Casey. Not in anger or any other way. And he wasn't at all sure what to do with the feelings that seeing her in danger had brought to the surface.

CHAPTER FOURTEEN

NICK AND CASEY didn't get back from the hospital until very late. But Casey was wired and shaky, and she couldn't have slept on a bet.

"Will you stay?" she asked Nick when they arrived at the cottage. On the way, they had passed the big house, dark, silent, brooding—looking like some gothic mansion in the fleeting moonlight.

Realizing her brother would hear the sirens when the police came, Casey had called and let Jackson know what had happened. He'd come to the hospital, as well, despite Casey's insistence that she was all right. She'd finally convinced him to go home after he'd been reassured by the doctor that neither she nor Nick had suffered serious injury.

But Esme hadn't showed up at all, which shouldn't have bothered her, but did. She was a grown woman who certainly didn't need her auntie taking care of her...especially not an aunt who was still furious with her.

"I should let you get some sleep," Nick said. He

wouldn't look at her. In fact, if she'd been the paranoid type, she'd have thought he was avoiding her.

"Nick, I—" She didn't want to seem weak and whining. But she felt vulnerable. And very, very lonely. Too lonely to let pride get in the way. "I really don't want to be by myself right now."

He didn't say anything, just turned off the car and got out. He'd been remarkably quiet since that moment in her office. Had she imagined what she'd seen in his eyes? She didn't believe so. But he sure didn't give the impression he wanted to talk about it now.

So she wouldn't talk. Instead, she took his hand and led him to her bedroom. Made him sit on her bed, stepped between his legs and started to unbutton his shirt. He still said nothing, just watched her with wary eyes. She kissed him and had the satisfaction of seeing the wariness fade a little.

Casey pushed his shirt off his shoulders, shuddering when she saw the bruises on his ribs, and the abrasions on his face and forearms from all the glass. She traced his ribs with her fingers. "I'm sorry. I knew he hurt you. It looks so painful." She leaned down and kissed him.

"Just bruises," he said, his voice hoarse. "Not even a cracked rib. I'll live."

"I know." She drew back and looked into his eyes. "So will I, thanks to you."

His eyes darkened, his lips tightened. "What were you thinking, going after that guy by yourself? He's three times your size."

"I didn't think. I just reacted." She bit her lip, glanced away from him. "I know it was stupid. I realized that when he—when he nearly—" She broke off, unwilling to complete the sentence.

"Yes, it was—"

He cupped the back of her neck and pulled her head down to put his lips on her bruised throat. She felt his tongue tracing each fingerprint, salving the hurt.

"Don't ever do that again. Don't ever put yourself in that kind of danger." He leaned back to look at her, his hands framing her face. "For a minute, when I walked in and saw his hands around your throat, I thought he'd killed you. Do you know how that made me feel?"

"No," she whispered. "Tell me."

"Scared. Bone scared." He tugged her down on the bed beside him. "I've never been that scared before. Not even when I was a kid and she left me—" He halted and started again. "I've never worried about another person, not like that. If I hadn't come in when I did—"

She stopped him with her fingers on his lips. "But you did. And I'm fine."

"I know," he murmured, and kissed her. "I

know.'' He held her as if he'd never let her go. He kissed her and lay down with her on the bed, his lips never leaving hers.

With frantic hands and trembling fingers, they helped each other out of their clothes, racing to feel bare skin against bare skin. She felt as if she were drowning, drowning in Nick.

She straddled him, and he put his hands on her hips to steady her. Then he tugged her head down to kiss her mouth. His tongue made long, slow, intense thrusts, as he slid inside her with the same rhythm. His hands tightened on her hips, helping her rise and fall with each deep thrust.

The light thrown by her bedside lamp was dim, but she could see every expression on his face clearly. She thought then that she would never forget this moment, no matter what came afterward. Their eyes met. His hands came up to her breasts, and she covered them with hers. He drove into her hard, just as she climaxed. He said her name, thrust one last time and shuddered as he came.

She didn't know how long she lay collapsed on his chest. It was a mistake, she knew that even before she said it, but she couldn't seem to help herself. Propping herself up on her forearms, she gazed down at him. He didn't look happy. If it hadn't sounded melodramatic, she'd have said he looked…tortured.

"Nick—"

"Casey, don't."

She said it anyway. "I love you."

He closed his eyes. "Don't say it."

"Why?"

He rolled them over, so he was above her. "I care about you, Casey. More than I've ever cared about any woman. More than I knew it was possible to care for a woman."

She stroked her fingers down his cheek. He looked so sad it almost broke her heart. "Nick, are you trying to say you love me?"

He shook his head. "I'm trying my best not to say it."

"I don't understand."

"I know. And I don't want to explain. Not now."

"Why?" she asked again.

He put a hand on her hair, gently caressing. "Because you said you didn't want to be alone tonight." He bent and kissed her lips. "And neither do I."

"And you think if we talked…" His tongue circled her nipple, then he sucked it deep into his mouth. His hand slid down between her legs, to stroke, to entice. Her back arched and she gasped, shivering at the liquid sensation that pooled between her legs. "Oh, I can't think when you do that."

"I know," he murmured against her breast. "Don't think. Just feel. We'll talk tomorrow." He

raised his head and gazed deep into her eyes. "Give me tonight, Casey. This one night."

It was a mistake. But she let him hold her, make love to her, and she couldn't regret it.

NICK DIDN'T REGRET the night before. How could he, when he knew it was the last time he'd ever make love to Casey? No, he didn't regret it, but he wished like hell the morning after hadn't come.

Nick had never had the luxury of ignoring reality. Not even when he was an infant, he suspected. His only recollections of his parents were of screaming, and fists, and pain. And hunger. Always hunger. Maybe there had been something else, but he had blocked that from his mind as surely as he'd blocked everything else. The past was dead, thank God, and he didn't intend to relive it.

He left Casey sleeping and went to make coffee. He didn't look forward to the conversation they were about to have. There were things he should have told her last night. He should never have made love to her without talking to her...but he hadn't been able to resist her. He'd come so close to losing her, in a very final way, and he'd needed to reassure himself that she was alive and well.

Maybe he was wrong. Maybe they did stand a chance. He could stick around and...and what? He closed his eyes and shook his head. Who was he

kidding? He knew nothing about families, nothing about love. Nothing about being there for another person, day in, day out, year in, year out. It wouldn't work—no matter how much he wished it would. And he owed it to Casey to tell her that.

He opened his eyes and saw her in front of him, wearing nothing but his shirt, her hair mussed, her eyes still sleepy. It was all he could do not to take her back to the bedroom and make love to her. To still the voices in his mind, to still the doubts.

But he couldn't. "Do you have to go to work?" he asked, instead.

She lifted a shoulder and yawned. "Yes, but not until later. I have time."

"I made coffee. Want me to get you a cup?"

"Thanks." She came over to him, put her arms around his waist and leaned her head against his chest. "Tell me what's wrong."

He put her away from him, poured coffee into a mug for her and refilled his own. "Come on, let's go sit down."

Casey followed him into the den, sat on the couch and sipped her coffee. After several minutes she said, "I'm getting the distinct impression you're about to dump me."

He shook his head, though he knew that was how this would seem. How could he explain his feelings to her when he couldn't explain them to himself?

How could he expect her to understand when he had no choice but to withhold that hidden part of himself? If he told Casey the truth, all of the truth, she would leave him, anyway. Just as his parents had.

So he would tell her some of the truth. The part he'd never been able to bury. But the rest would stay inside him, locked in that dark corner of his mind. "It's not that simple. I wish it were, but it isn't."

He cupped his hands around his mug, trying to decide what to say and how best to say it. She didn't speak, but he could feel her gaze on him, warm and questioning.

"I told you I grew up in an orphanage. From the time I was seven." She nodded and he went on. "I stayed until I was fifteen, because I wanted my GED and knew I wouldn't get it if I left. Besides, at that age my options were very limited. But there wasn't a day that went by that I didn't wish like hell that I was somewhere else."

"Were they— Did they abuse you?"

"No." He smiled. "Don't be envisioning Oliver Twist. They fed us, took care of us. But no one loved us. It just—" he spread his hands "—wasn't that kind of place. And the friendships you made there, well, they didn't last, either. You never knew who would leave next. Who would get in trouble with the law, or run away. A few kids even got

adopted. Not many, but some. The rest of us really hated them.''

"It sounds depressing.''

"It was.'' He got up and went to the kitchen to refill their mugs. He handed hers to her and sat beside her again. "I spent eight years there. That's the longest I ever stayed anywhere, but it wasn't a home. I've never had a home.''

"Does it bother you? Not having a home?''

"It hasn't. Until now.'' He put down his mug and took her hands, carrying each one to his mouth. "I didn't expect what happened between us, Casey. I thought we'd have a brief, mutually satisfying relationship and then I'd move on and so would you.'' He squeezed her hands, looked into those green eyes that glistened like pools. "That isn't what happened.''

"That's all I thought it would be, too. At first. But that changed for me. And it didn't take long.''

It hadn't taken him long, either. He'd started falling for her the first time he'd kissed her. "I fell in love with you, Casey. Which I didn't expect. Hell, I'm thirty-six years old and I've never fallen in love before. I didn't figure I ever would. Didn't think I could.''

He was still holding her hands, still wishing he didn't have to end their relationship. But anything

else would only hurt her more, and he felt like a bastard as it was.

"So what's the problem? Isn't the fact that I love you and you love me the most important thing here?" she asked him. "I don't understand why you're so upset."

"Because it doesn't matter. It's not going to work."

"Love matters. And why wouldn't it work?"

"Love won't change anything. It won't change my past."

"But it could change our future. If you let it," she said softly.

God, how he wished he could believe that. But he didn't. "I've never stayed in a place longer than a few months in my adult life. I've never wanted to."

She gazed at him for a moment before understanding flashed in her eyes. "Oh, I get it. You still don't want to."

"Yes, I want to. But damn it, Casey, I don't believe I can." He got up and started to pace. "It's not a matter of wanting or not wanting." He wanted her, all right. More than he'd wanted anything in his life. But he couldn't have her. "I don't know if I can do it. I'm just not put together that way. And the longer I stay here, the longer I stay with you,

the harder it's going to be for us when the end in-evitably comes.''

''Why is it inevitable?''

''Because I'll let you down. I've never had a fam-ily. Never been responsible for anyone. To anyone. I've never even had a dog or a cat. How am I sup-posed to believe that I can settle down? Be counted on?''

She got up and gazed down at him, her arms folded across her chest. ''So that's it? You're not even willing to try?''

''I'm not willing to hurt you any more than I al-ready have.''

''Give me a break. You're scared, that's what this is about.''

That stung. And angered him. Couldn't she see how this was hurting him? Did she think he was enjoying himself? ''Damn it, I'm trying to do the right thing. The best thing for you.'' And all she could do was hassle him.

''Bullshit,'' she said in disgust. ''If you want to walk away, don't kid yourself you're doing it for me. You're walking because you don't have the guts to see it through.''

''If that's what you believe—''

''That's exactly what I believe.'' Her fingers had been busy with the shirt buttons. With that, she un-did the last one, stripped the shirt off and threw it

at him. ''Go away, Nick. And don't let the door hit you in the ass on the way out.'' She turned on her heel and stalked out.

A moment later he heard a door slam. He got up and stood there, shocked at how suddenly the situation had deteriorated.

He started to go, then realized both his keys and his shoes were in Casey's bedroom. Something told him she wouldn't take kindly to him knocking on the door. Before he made up his mind what to do, she appeared in the doorway—wearing a T-shirt now—tossed his shoes and keys in his direction and turned her back again without saying a word.

He wanted to go after her. Wanted to tell her he loved her, wanted to hear her say she loved him, one final time. Instead, he walked out the door.

CHAPTER FIFTEEN

THE NEXT FEW DAYS dragged by for Casey. The only good thing was that she was incredibly busy with the harvest. Nothing was certain, but there was still a chance they'd come out of the whole mess not too badly damaged.

But she wasn't so busy that she didn't have plenty of time to think about Nick, and their last conversation. When Jordan had jilted her she'd thought that was the worst pain she'd ever have to face, but it hadn't even come close to what she felt when Nick broke it off between them.

She reached for the phone a dozen times, only to stop herself just as many. What could she say in the face of such irrational behavior? He'd admitted he loved her, and he knew she loved him. Yet he still meant to throw away everything they might have together. Because of his past.

Love couldn't change his past. There was obviously a lot he wasn't telling her, because she couldn't see the reason for his behavior, given what little he'd told her. She didn't understand why being

an orphan meant he had to go through life alone, but that was apparently what Nick believed.

The big dummy.

Earlier that morning, Casey had gotten a phone call from Megan, inviting her to lunch today. There was no way she could refuse, and besides, she wanted to see the little girl. Even though Esme would be there, ready to gloat over the fact that her prediction about Nick and Casey had come true.

Casey didn't believe for a moment that anyone in the big house didn't know that she and Nick were no longer an item. Probably everyone in Baton Rouge knew. Certainly all the single women would know, she thought glumly.

But she wouldn't disappoint Megan just because it made her uncomfortable to see her aunt, so she squared her shoulders and set off for Bellefontaine. She'd been out in the fields all morning, and as luck would have it, she'd forgotten her hat and had never had a chance to go back and get it. The sun was high and heat shimmered in waves off the dirt road, the dry dust rising with each step, making her cough.

Her vision blurred and her head started to spin. She shook her head, wishing she'd thought to drink some water when she'd come in from the fields. She glanced at Bellefontaine, gauging the distance. A few hundred yards. Once she had some water, she'd feel better.

Each footstep became progressively harder to take. She felt as if she were swimming in cement. Black dots danced in front of her eyes. A roaring sounded in her ears, and the dots merged into a curtain. She staggered, went down on her knees and then crumpled.

She came to when someone threw a glass of water in her face. Flat on her back, she gazed up at Betty and Esme.

"She needs to drink it, not have it thrown in her face," Esme said in a superior tone. "Any fool would know that."

"Humph," Betty said, crossing her arms over her chest and dangling a plastic pitcher from her hand. "Well, this fool can see that she's come to. So put that in your pipe and smoke it."

Esme ignored her and knelt down beside Casey, offering her a glass of water. "Here, let me help you." She put her arm behind her and got her to a sitting position.

"I— What happened?" she asked Esme as she obediently sipped the liquid. "Last thing I knew I was walking along the road and then…" She wrinkled her brow, but nothing more came. "That's it. That's all I remember."

"You fainted," Esme said. "From the heat." She glared at Betty, as if daring her to say differently.

"We'll see about that," Betty said ominously.

"From the heat," Esme repeated. "Now, give her a hand. She needs to get out of this sun. It's a wonder we're not all lying in the dirt."

"I'm all right," Casey said, embarrassed. "I can get up by myself."

"Don't be foolish," Esme said, and for once, Betty nodded agreement.

She didn't faint. She never fainted. Well, she'd passed out during the fire because of smoke inhalation, but she wasn't the fainting type.

Esme and Betty each held a hand and pulled her to her feet, one remaining on either side of her. "I can walk fine," she protested. "I can't imagine what happened."

Betty snorted but didn't speak. Esme simply took her arm and walked toward the back porch.

Once inside, they forced her to sit on the couch. She gave in, first because she was no match for two determined Southern women, and second, because she was afraid she'd fall down if she didn't. "I'm supposed to be having lunch with Megan. Where is she?"

"I'll tell her you're not feeling well. You can see her when you're steadier," Esme said.

"No, don't do that. I'll be all right in a minute. I don't want to disappoint her."

Oddly enough, Esme didn't argue. "All right, but

first, you need more liquid. Betty, get her some orange juice.''

''Orange juice is well and good, but she needs
food, I'll wager. When's the last time you ate, girl?''

Casey shrugged. The past few days she'd been
living on coffee and nerves. Besides, her appetite
had deserted her the same day Nick left.

''I knew it.'' Betty moved to the stove, muttering
darkly.

Esme came back a short time later, leading Megan
by the hand. Betty served the two of them at the
table, a hurried meal of toast and eggs, while Esme
took a seat in one of the armchairs, her little silver-
coated dog at her feet.

Casey smiled as she listened to Megan's account
of what had happened at preschool the day before.
Megan was settling in, feeling more comfortable
with the family. Even a few weeks earlier, she
hadn't chattered so much.

As soon as they finished, Megan went off to find
Tanya. Casey looked at her aunt and waited to see
what she'd say. She didn't think Esme was through
with her yet.

At least she felt better now that she had something
in her stomach. What an idiot she'd been not to eat,
she thought, more than a little embarrassed.

''Now, then,'' Esme said after Megan left, clearly

gearing up for a long visit. "I'm sure Betty will be happy to do the dishes later."

"Betty won't do any such thing," she said, walking over to them with the spatula still in hand. "I raised her the same as you did. Who fed this family for the past thirty-some years? Who listened to this child cry when that no-account Whittaker boy broke her heart, when you and her mother wouldn't spare her the time of day?"

"That's not your place to say," Esme said, flushing. "Angelique wanted to talk to her, she...simply didn't have the words. Why would you even bring that up?"

"It needed saying," Betty stated grimly.

"Well, it didn't need saying right this minute. I have private things to say to my niece. *Solitude, s'il vous plaît.*"

"Private, my eye. If you think you can tell me to go on about my business just like I'm the hired help and not a part of this family—"

"Betty, of course Aunt Esme didn't mean that. You know you're family." First a near heatstroke, now a family feud.

Casey hadn't realized until this moment how much it had hurt that her mother hadn't supported her when Jordan jilted her. Angelique had faded into the woodwork, just as she always did when something upsetting happened. It was a failing of hers.

Now that Casey was grown, she recognized it as such. It didn't mean her mother didn't love her, it simply meant she wasn't capable of handling that kind of emotion. But knowing that hadn't helped when she'd been heartbroken.

"Look, I'm fine. Neither of you needs to worry. I'm very grateful you saw me out there and came to get me, but nothing's wrong that a little rest and cool air won't fix. I worked out in the fields all morning and I didn't drink enough water."

"Cassandra, are you pregnant?"

Casey felt as if her eyes were popping out of her head. She'd never expected that question from the prim and proper Esme. She glanced at Betty, but saw no support there.

"Well?" Betty said. "Are you?"

"Of course I'm not pregnant. Why would you even think that?"

Betty snorted. "Could be because we're not stupid, Casey. Everyone knows what's been going on between you and that Nick Devlin. And now you faint dead away in the middle of the road, when you've never done such a thing in your life. What are we supposed to think?"

If she hadn't been so miserable, she'd have laughed at their identical stern expressions. "You can think that *I* was stupid. I haven't been eating, and then today I didn't drink enough water. It was

the heat, mostly. I'm not pregnant.'' Of course she wasn't pregnant. She was stressed, that was all.

Esme laid her hand over Casey's, surprising her. ''If you are, we'll face it together.''

Casey stared at her. In light of the grief Esme had given Jackson over his illegitimate daughter, she couldn't imagine her aunt softening toward her. Especially not considering the scandal it would be bound to cause if two Fontaines had illegitimate children.

''Did you know Nick and I broke up? A few days ago?''

Esme nodded grimly. ''We know.''

''Everybody does,'' Betty added. ''Don't you worry, honey, we'll make him see reason.''

''I'm touched. No, I truly am,'' she said, when Esme frowned. ''I appreciate the support more than you can know. But I'm not pregnant. You don't have to worry, okay?''

Toodles jumped up on the couch beside her and licked her hand. Casey looked at him, then her aunt. ''I thought he hated me? What's going on?''

''Don't be foolish, Cassandra. Toodles doesn't hate anyone in the family.''

Hesitantly she patted his head. Lord, even the dog was surprising her today.

''Betty, would you please let me talk to Cassandra alone? I have something to say to her that I think

she needs to know. And you're already aware of the story.''

Betty pursed her lips and gazed at Esme before giving a brisk nod. '''Bout time you told her,'' she said, and left the room.

Casey stared after Betty, amazed at the exchange. She turned to her aunt. ''It sounds like you're about to tell me a deep, dark secret. I didn't know we had any skeletons in the closet.''

''All families do. Even the Fontaines,'' Esme said. ''I should have told you years ago. Especially when Jordan…jilted you. But I was ashamed and I wanted to pretend nothing had happened to me. So I didn't speak of it.''

''Tell me what, Aunt Esme?''

''You didn't just faint from the heat, did you?'' She held up a hand when Casey started to reiterate that she wasn't pregnant. ''You haven't been eating, you haven't been sleeping. You look miserable. And I know why. Your heart's been broken, more than it ever was by Jordan Whittaker.''

Casey closed her eyes. Exactly what she'd been dreading. ''Aunt Esme, I'm just not up to hearing you rant about Nick.''

''I'm not going to rant about him.''

Casey opened her eyes. ''You're not?''

Esme shook her head. ''I shouldn't have before.

You're old enough to know what you want. Or who.''

"If that's how you really feel, then why were you so hard on me?"

"I wanted to keep you from getting hurt. Probably because—'' she bit her lip ''—I know what you're going through right now.''

Casey didn't say anything. Because of veiled references from time to time, she had suspected something bad had happened in Esme's past. But she'd never been able to find out what.

"When I was eighteen I fell in love with the most wonderful man in the world. I thought he loved me. He said he did. He asked me to marry him. We were young, and I was in school, so we planned to marry my sophomore year. I asked a friend of mine from school—you know, from the Sorbonne—to come home with me for winter break. She was going to be in my wedding party, and I wanted to introduce her to my family and my fiancé. She came to stay with me for several weeks.'' Her gaze met Casey's. "My friend was your mother, Angelique.''

"That's when Duke and Maman met and fell in love? When you brought her home with you from school?''

"Yes. Your father took one look at Angelique and fell madly in love with her. And so did someone else.''

Casey gasped.

Esme nodded. "That's right. My fiancé."

"Oh, Aunt Esme, how awful for you. What happened?"

"He jilted me. He told me—" She twisted her hands together in her lap and bowed her head. "He said he'd never loved me. He only wanted me because the Fontaines had money and prestige."

"What a bastard."

Esme looked up with the glimmer of a smile. "*Mais, oui.* I've always thought so." She sighed and continued. "After he jilted me he continued to come around, to see Angelique. He refused to accept that she was in love with Duke. He seemed to think that if he persevered, Angelique would choose him. Of course, she didn't." This time Esme's smile was a satisfied one. "Do you know he even had the gall to ask me to marry him again, once Angelique had married your father? As if nothing had ever happened."

"I hope you laughed in his face."

"Not quite," she said primly. "I told him I'd rather chew off my leg than be trapped in a loveless marriage with the likes of him. Then I had your father escort him out." She folded her hands together, the epitome of proper Southern womanhood. "You know I have never approved of fisticuffs, but

that was one time I was pleased with my brother's violent tendencies.''

Casey could well imagine Duke wiping the floor with Esme's erstwhile suitor. ''Who was he, Aunt Esme? Anyone I know?''

''Oh, yes.'' She nodded. ''Roland Dewalt.''

Shock had her eyes widening. ''Roland Dewalt? Oh my God, I'd never… So that's the reason for the feud. Does Murray know?''

''I have no idea. I've scarcely spoken to Roland since the day he asked me to marry him the second time.''

''Good lord, Roland Dewalt. I can't imagine how you've even been civil to him all these years.''

''One does what one must,'' Esme said with gentle dignity. ''I am a Fontaine, after all.''

''I'm so sorry. I'm glad you told me, but I'm so sorry it happened.''

''I wanted you to know that I understand what you're feeling right now. I was very much in love with him, even though he turned out to be a cad.''

''Nick isn't. He isn't like that. He admitted he loved me, and I believe him.''

''Then, why aren't you together?''

Casey groaned. Good question. Very good question. ''I don't know. Because he's— I think he's scared. No, I know he is. It's got something to do

with his past, with being an orphan. With never having had a home.''

''Perhaps you should talk to him.''

Casey nodded. ''I intend to. Once I figure out what I want to say.'' She got to her feet, bent down and kissed her aunt's cheek. ''Thank you for telling me your story, Aunt Esme. It means a lot to me that you did.''

Esme grasped her hand, her eyes suspiciously bright. ''I don't want us to be at odds, Cassandra.''

''We're not. Not anymore.'' She smiled at her aunt.

Then, hearing a sound, she glanced at the doorway. Jackson stood there, his face a ghastly white.

Casey went to him, lay a hand on his arm. ''Jackson, what is it? What's wrong?''

''Maman and Duke.'' His voice sounded strangled. He cleared his throat, gazing at her with tortured eyes. ''There's been an accident.''

''An accident? Maman and Duke? Are they hurt? What happened? They're not—'' She put her hand up to still her galloping heart.

Jackson nodded, his throat working. ''They're dead, Casey. Their jet crashed in the Italian Alps.''

CHAPTER SIXTEEN

"WHAT? MAMAN AND DUKE? They're...dead?"
Her parents were dead? They couldn't be. "No, I
don't believe it. There must be some mistake."

Jackson shook his head. "I'm afraid...there's no
mistake. I just got off the phone with the authorities
in Cortina, Italy."

Casey heard a choked sound and looked at Esme.
She'd buried her face in her hands. Still in shock,
Casey walked over and put her hand on her aunt's
shoulder. To give her strength? Or to draw some for
herself?

"Come sit down, Jackson, and tell us what you
know." She didn't cry, because she couldn't believe
what he had said was real.

"Damn little." He sat down heavily on the couch.
"The authorities said Duke and Maman were sight-
seeing. Duke was at the controls." He smiled
weakly. "You know how Duke loved to fly. Anytime he got a chance, he took it."

"I know," Casey said, remembering going up
with him when she was young. "Go on."

"There's not much more. Yet, anyway." He spoke slowly, hesitantly. As if each word was an effort. "Duke had fired Chuck Riley, their relief pilot, but no one seems clear as to why. We'll know more when the authorities do. Once they've had a chance to investigate the wreckage."

Casey left her aunt and sat down by Jackson, taking his hand and offering support in the only way she could. "Go on."

"About an hour into the flight, Duke placed a Mayday to the airport they'd flown out of, and that's the last that was heard from them. That call helped pinpoint the location of the crash. Fortunately, it was in an accessible place. A few miles to the east and authorities wouldn't have been able to reach the site for days or even weeks."

"Did they— Did they suffer?" Esme asked, speaking for the first time since Jackson had told them the news. Esme had aged in the past few minutes. Her eyes looked haunted and glistened with the sheen of tears.

Jackson reached over and took her hand. "The authorities believe Maman and Duke died on impact, Aunt Esme."

"So they didn't suffer." Esme drew in a shaky breath. "At least we have that comfort."

Comfort? Casey didn't feel comforted. She was

numb. How could such a thing be true? Her parents gone?

"Jackson, are they positive? Maybe— Maybe they couldn't identify the bodies. Maybe it was a mistake and they got these people mixed up with Maman and Duke...."

He shook his head, slowly. "They were positively identified. There's no mistake. They're gone, Casey," he said gently.

And that's when she believed the news, looking into her brother's grief-filled eyes. Their parents were dead. She put her head on Jackson's shoulder and the tears fell.

NICK WAS NOT having a good day. Guy Moreau was nowhere to be found, leaving Nick to handle a lot of details that shouldn't have been his problem at this point. He was beginning to wonder what he'd got himself into. Three cocktail waitresses had quit for varying reasons. A chef had been fired. And one of the captains had just told him that another floating casino had offered him a substantial pay raise if he changed ships. All Nick needed now was for Luc's band to leave.

And, of course, there was Casey. He couldn't get her out of his mind. He knew he'd done the right thing, so why did he feel like such a heel? Why did

he still want her so badly it was like a physical ache? One no painkiller on earth could dull.

He opened his desk drawer and took out the list of job applicants. He hadn't gotten far when a knock sounded on his office door. "Come in," he said without looking up.

He finished the line he was reading and glanced at his visitor. Viv Renault stood in front of his desk. She didn't speak, she just stared at him. "Don't tell me," he said. "Luc broke his arm and won't be able to play for a month."

"It's not Luc." She put out a hand and grasped the back of a chair, her knuckles whitening. "It's Casey."

He jumped up and was at her side in two strides, grasping her arm. "What happened? Is she all right?"

Viv nodded. "She's all right." She closed her eyes and shook her head. "What am I saying? Of course she's not. She's terrible, I'm sure. Nick, Casey's parents were killed in a plane crash in Italy. They just got word today."

He released her arm, his heart rate slowing down. Thank God Casey was all right. But her parents… "When did you hear?"

"Just now. Casey called me. I'm going out to Bellefontaine. I thought you would want to go with me."

He wanted to, but what comfort could he offer Casey or Jackson? A man who hadn't seen his parents in nearly thirty years, who didn't even know if they were alive or dead, and what's more, didn't care. Worse, the man who had broken Casey's heart. No, neither she nor Jackson would want him there.

He shook his head. ''I don't think Casey will want to see me.''

''Of course she will. She needs you. And so does Jackson.''

He wanted to be there, wanted to help, though he knew there wasn't much he could do. ''You know Casey and I broke up. I might just make things worse.''

''And you might bring her, and Jackson, some comfort.'' Her brown eyes darkened with sympathy.

He nodded. ''All right. Let me get my keys.'' If he could help…he owed it to both Jackson and Casey to try. Besides, Casey could always throw him out if she wanted him gone.

BETTY OPENED THE DOOR. Her eyes and nose were red and she clutched a tissue in her hand. The eternal cigarette was stuck behind her ear, instead of dangling from her mouth. She looked terribly sad and haggard.

She made a choked sound and gathered Viv into

a hug. "Oh, Betty, I'm so sorry," Viv said a few minutes later. "How are they?"

Betty just shook her head. "Esme's lying down. Never thought I'd see the day I felt sorry for Miss Froufrou, but there it is. She did love the two of them, I'll say that for her."

"Where are Casey and Jackson?"

"They're both on the back porch." She gave Nick a long, baleful glare. "Don't know as how Casey will be happy to see you."

"If she isn't, I'll leave," Nick said. But he had to make the effort. Why he'd ever thought he could stay away when she might need him, he didn't know.

Betty studied him sharply, then nodded. "Fair enough."

They found Casey on the porch, but Jackson was nowhere to be seen. She was standing looking out over the lawn, arms crossed over her chest.

Viv said her name softly. She turned around, her expression surprised when she saw Nick. She didn't speak, she just looked at them both with more anguish in her eyes than Nick had ever seen. He wanted to help, wanted to comfort. He just didn't know how.

Viv didn't seem to have that problem. She folded Casey in her arms, and they both cried. After a bit, Casey drew back and smiled weakly. "Thanks for

coming, Viv.'' She sniffed and wiped her eyes with her fingers. ''I wish I had a tissue. I used up a box already.''

Viv smiled and dug in her purse. ''Here,'' she said, presenting her with a packet. ''You never have one when you need it.'' She looked from Nick to Casey while Casey was blotting her eyes and blowing her nose. ''Where's Jackson?''

''In the study. He said he needed to be alone. But he's been in there an hour or more. Will you go talk to him, Viv?''

''Of course. I'll tell him you're here, Nick,'' she said, and left the room.

Casey looked at Nick. ''I'm glad you came,'' she said simply.

''I'm sorry.'' It hurt him to see her so miserable, particularly when he couldn't help. And that had been his problem most of his life, he realized. When it came to business, he was damn good at trouble-shooting. But let things get personal and he had no idea what to do. And he hated being powerless. ''I wish there was something I could do.''

''There is,'' she said, and walked into his arms. ''Just hold me.''

Nick wished he were a different kind of man. Wished he could stay with Casey and love her and build a future with her. He wished he could, but he didn't *believe* he could. Despite that, she needed him

now. Right now, not in the future. So he stroked her back until he felt some of the tension leave her. A long time later, Casey drew back and led him to the couch.

"Do you feel like talking about it?" He probably wouldn't, in such circumstances, but women were different. It made them feel better to talk.

"I don't know. Not really," she said, but after a few seconds she did. "We don't know much beyond the bare facts. They died in a plane crash in the Italian Alps. My father was the pilot. Jackson's trying to find out more, but so far he hasn't been able to."

"Maybe they'll know more tomorrow."

"I don't know, I hope so. It's hard with it happening in Europe, and us being here." She was silent for a moment, her fingers plucking at the couch fabric in a nervous gesture totally alien to her. "I've been wondering if it would be easier if I still had one of them. But I think… No, I *know* if they had chosen, they'd have wanted to go together."

She glanced at Nick and smiled weakly. "They loved each other so much. One would have been lost without the other. They each had their own lives, their own interests, but at the heart of it, they were together. Bonded. They'd been married thirty-three years. Can you imagine being married to one person so long?"

He knew it was a rhetorical question, but he answered, anyway. "No." He couldn't imagine having parents, much less parents who'd been together a lifetime.

"Oh, that's right. You don't believe love can last, do you? Or that it can change your life."

"Not everyone is like your parents, Casey. They're the exception, rather than the rule."

"How do you know?" she asked, obviously growing angry. "You've never stayed in one place long enough to find out, have you?"

Her words hurt, even though she was speaking the truth. Or maybe because she spoke the truth. "No, I haven't. And I've never seen anything like what you're describing. My parents dumped me in an orphanage when I was seven, remember?"

She stared at him aghast, then put out her hand. "Oh, God, Nick. I'm sorry, I shouldn't have said anything. I'm just so upset, I didn't think what I was saying. I took my feelings out on you."

"It doesn't matter. You're right. All this—" he gestured at the house "—your family, your parents, your home. It's all strange to me. Something I've never had, something I can't understand."

She took his hand and squeezed it. "I'm sorry."

He shrugged. "Don't be. You can't miss what you've never had."

"Can't you?"

He didn't know how to answer that, so he remained silent. A few moments later, she spoke again, changing the subject. "Duke didn't really want to go on this trip. Not for such an extended time. But Maman insisted. She said it would be a second honeymoon. No one ever expected it to end like this." She was quiet for a moment, then continued. "We talked to them, every so often. I've never heard my father sound so relaxed. I didn't know he could be, didn't know he could survive without his business for that long."

She gazed at Nick, her eyes filling with tears. "I guess he didn't have to, did he?"

He didn't say anything, he just put his arm around her and held her as she cried.

A little while later Viv and Jackson joined them. Nick got up, shook Jackson's hand and said the only thing he could think of, useless as it seemed. "I'm sorry about your parents."

"Thanks," Jackson said. "I'm glad you came."

"If I can do anything…"

"Maybe you and Viv could keep Casey company a while. I need to look through some paperwork and I don't think Casey's up to it."

"What paperwork, Jackson?" Casey asked. "I can help if you need me to."

He shook his head. "No, that's all right. It's the policy to allow us to bring Duke and Maman home.

It's in Duke's files somewhere. It's just a matter of looking.''

''Be sure and call me if you need me,'' Casey said.

So the three of them sat and talked a little, mostly Viv and Casey sharing reminiscences about the elder Fontaines. After a while Betty came in and fixed them something to eat, which Viv and Nick ate but Casey only picked at.

About an hour after he'd left, Jackson returned. He didn't look as if he was grieving. Nick would have said he looked stunned.

''Casey, I need to see you alone. Can you come to the study with me?''

''Did you hear from the authorities again? I've heard the phone ringing off the walls.''

''No, nothing. It's about—'' He hesitated. ''It's private. I need to talk to you.''

''Nick and I will leave,'' Viv said. ''You call us if you need us, okay?''

Casey nodded.

''I'll be with you in a minute, Viv,'' Nick said.

Viv walked out. Nick hesitated, not wanting to leave Casey. But he'd given up his right to stay when he'd told Casey it was over between them. ''I'll be around if you need me.'' He gave her a last hug and left.

Viv was at the front entrance, waiting for him. "Can you give me a ride home?"

"Sure. Where's Luc?"

"He's been with his brothers. He said he'd come by later. He doesn't know the family as well as I do, so he wanted to give me some time with them before he came over."

"They must have told Adam, too. I don't see any workmen around."

They reached his car and he opened the door for her.

"Nick, can you figure out what that was about? I've never seen Jackson look like that. So shocked. They just found out their parents are dead. What could be worse than that?"

Nick shook his head. "I have no idea, but Jackson sure as hell wanted us gone."

CHAPTER SEVENTEEN

"WHY DID YOU RUN Nick and Viv off like that?"
Casey asked Jackson once they were in their father's
office. "I know you're upset but you were down-
right rude."

Her brother took a seat in Duke's chair. It hurt to
realize she'd never see their father sit there again.

"I had my reasons. And I wasn't rude, I just
needed to see you alone."

"What is this about?"

"It's about this—" he said, holding up a piece of
paper. "And these—" He set the paper down and
picked up a bundle of letters. "I found them in
Duke's files when I was looking for the policy to—
to bring them back to the States."

She shied away from that subject, not wanting to
think about that. Instead she concentrated on the paper her brother had held up. "This is a birth certificate." Frowning, she glanced at Jackson. "I don't
understand."

"Read it," he said, his voice devoid of emotion.

She read aloud. "Baby girl, Noelani Hana, born

October 8, 1975, at Wailuku Memorial in Wailuku, Maui, Hawaii. Mother, Anela Hana. Father, unknown.'' She looked back to her brother. ''So?''

''These letters—'' he held up the bundle ''—are addressed to Anela Hana in Hawaii. They're from our father. They were returned to him, unopened. They're postmarked twenty-eight years ago.''

Her stomach hurt, though she wasn't sure why. ''What are you trying to say, Jackson?''

''Isn't it obvious? Noelani Hana is our half sister.''

''Are you crazy? How can you—? She's only a few months younger than you are. That would mean Duke…that he—'' She was unable to finish that thought. ''How can you even think such a thing of our father?''

''For God's sake, don't act like I want to believe it. I don't. But it's the obvious conclusion, and one we can easily validate. Don't take my word for it— open the letters and read them.''

She reached out to take one, anxious to prove him wrong. Her hand dropped. But what if Jackson was right? ''I can't. You do it.''

Jackson picked up one of the letters and slit the envelope open. ''This is the last one. I'll start with it first.'' He pulled out a sheet of paper and read, then shook his head and looked at her. ''Do you want to read it?''

"Do I need to?" She could tell by his expression that it was bad news.

"Yes." He handed her the letter and opened another one.

Casey began to read. As always, her father's handwriting was bold and decisive. Like the man himself.

My love,
I know now why you've refused my letters, why you felt you had no choice but to break off all contact with me. I received our daughter's birth certificate from Bruce Shiller yesterday. I wish you had told me. I wish I could have made another choice, but Angelique needs me. She gave birth to a son a few months before Noelani was born. I told her everything, and she has forgiven me. Now if I could only forgive myself for the pain I've caused two fine women.

I know you wish you'd never heard of me. I never intended to cause you heartbreak. I did love you, Anela. I always will. But my duty is to my family. Soon, God willing, my love will rekindle as well. I have arranged with Bruce to care for our child, and for you. Please don't refuse me this, at least. Raise our daughter

knowing that we loved each other very much, even though we weren't fated to remain together.

> With all my love,
> Duke

Casey closed her eyes and raised a clenched fist to her mouth. Her father had been unfaithful. Not only that, but he'd loved another woman. How could he have done it? How could her father have betrayed his family this way? Another woman? And even worse, he'd had the affair while her mother was pregnant with Jackson.

"Do you want to read any more?" Jackson asked.

Sickened, Casey shook her head. "I wish to God I hadn't read that one." She got up and started to pace. Grabbed a pillow off the couch and heaved it across the room. Her eyes lit on the crystal decanter and glasses. She started to grab a piece, but Jackson's voice stopped her.

"Don't even think about it. The last thing we need with Megan around is broken glass everywhere."

Casey gritted her teeth. He was right. "I can't believe it. I can't believe Duke would do such a thing. I thought he loved Maman."

"He did. You know he did." Jackson picked up the phone and punched in numbers.

"Who are you calling?" Casey asked.

"Shelburne Prescott," he said, referring to the family lawyer. "He'll know about this. Duke would have arranged everything through him. We need confirmation."

Casey didn't listen while her brother talked to the lawyer. She could hear nothing but the crash of her fantasy about her parents' marriage.

Jackson hung up the phone and rubbed the bridge of his nose. He looked exhausted, angry…grief-stricken. Everything Casey herself was feeling.

"Shelburne confirmed it. As far as he's aware, Aunt Esme doesn't know, either, so we'll have to tell her. He says there's a provision in the will for Noelani Hana, and she has to be notified of Duke's death. He wants to hold off on the formal reading until she arrives."

"Arrives? You mean here? That woman is coming here? To Bellefontaine?"

Jackson nodded. "I told him to put off sending for her until after the funeral. The last thing we need is for our father's illegitimate daughter to arrive during our parents' funeral."

"What did he leave her?" she asked abruptly.

Jackson spread his hands. "I don't know, but I have to admit I'm worried. We'll find out when she gets here, I guess."

And when their illegitimate sister arrived, would she tear the family—and Bellefontaine—apart?

Her parents were dead. Her father, whom she'd always adored, had been unfaithful. And he had an illegitimate daughter to prove it. "I just can't believe this."

"Neither can I. But I guess we'd better get used to it." They were both silent for a time, then Jackson said, "I'm going to call Italy now, and make arrangements to bring them home."

He stopped, closed his eyes and rubbed his forehead. "I don't understand this any more than you do. But I do know one thing. Maman forgave him, Casey. We have to remember that, and make our peace with it."

"Maman had a bigger heart than I do. I don't know if *I* can forgive him."

AFTER DROPPING VIV OFF at her house, Nick returned to the boat and spent a couple of hours trying to deal with the problems he'd been working on earlier. Guy still hadn't shown up. Finally, around midnight, Nick gave up and went back to the *garçonnière*.

Casey was sitting on his front step when he drove up. She stood when she saw him.

"Have you been waiting there long?" he asked her. "Why didn't you call me?"

"Not that long. I didn't mind waiting. It gave me a chance to think about some things."

He couldn't see her well in the dark, but her voice was thick and hoarse—from crying, he was sure. "Your parents?" he asked, and let her inside. "Did you hear anything else?"

"Yes, but not what you're thinking."

"Can I get you something to drink? Water?" She didn't look good. In fact, she looked like a gentle breeze would knock her over.

She shook her head, saying nothing. He did the only thing he could think of to comfort her. He took her in his arms and held her. "Do you want to talk about it?" he asked.

She slipped her arms around his waist. "I want it not to be true. But since it is…"

"Come on." He made her sit on the couch, then sat beside her. "Talk to me."

"You probably think I'm a fool. I mean, we're not even together and here I am, crying on your shoulder. But I can't help it. I have to talk to somebody, and you're the only one it won't hurt."

Not true, because whatever was hurting her hurt him, as well. But he was glad she'd come to him. "Casey. Talk to me," he repeated. "What's wrong? Something besides your parents' deaths?"

Biting her lip, she nodded, then took a deep breath. "Remember this afternoon when we were talking about my parents? And I said they'd had a wonderful marriage and I threw it in your face when

you said all marriages weren't like that, that my parents were the exception?"

He didn't have a clue where she was going with this. "I remember."

"The joke's on me," she said, and gave a humorless laugh. "It was a lie. I thought they had this perfect marriage. And every bit of it was a lie."

"Why do you say that?"

"Can I have some water?" she said abruptly. "I don't feel very well."

"Have you eaten anything today?"

"I ate some lunch."

And nothing since, he bet. He'd seen her picking at what Betty had brought in earlier. He went to pour her a glass of water and looked around the tiny kitchen for something to feed her. All he could find was some cheese and a box of undoubtedly stale crackers, so he brought that with him.

"Here."

She didn't comment, just ate a few crackers and a bit of cheese, then drank her water while he waited. When she finished she looked at him and said, "Jackson and I found out today that we have a half sister. Our father had an affair with a Hawaiian woman, and she had a child."

Nick winced. "That obviously came as a complete surprise to you."

Casey shook her head. "You could say that. No

one knew, other than my mother—not even Aunt Esme. Our family lawyer confirmed it. This woman— H-his daughter is only a few months younger than Jackson. Duke had an affair while my mother was pregnant. Who knows how many others he had or how many half siblings he's got stashed around, waiting to surprise us?''

''Just because it happened once—''

''Oh, please, spare me. The lawyer assured us this is Duke's only other offspring. That he knew about, anyway.'' She glared at Nick, her eyes bright with unshed tears. ''He did it once. Who's to say he didn't do it multiple times?''

''Do you really believe that?'' Nick hadn't known the man, but from what Casey and Jackson had said, Duke Fontaine hadn't sounded like a womanizer.

''I don't know what I believe!'' She clenched her fists, her voice anguished. ''I believed my parents loved each other. I believed they had a good marriage.'' She turned her head to gaze at Nick. ''My mother knew. She knew about his affair, knew about the child. In the letter, the last letter my father wrote to the other woman, he said he'd told Maman everything, and she had forgiven him.''

Tears sparkled in her eyes. He couldn't imagine how she was feeling, couldn't begin to see how he could help her.

"How could she forgive him? He betrayed her, he betrayed all of us."

"He stayed with you, didn't he?"

She paid no attention to the question. "He conceived a child with another woman. He talked about leaving my mother. About leaving…me."

Nick covered her hand with his. "But he didn't. He chose to stay with his family. Shouldn't that count for something?"

"Why should it? Who's to say it wasn't the easy way out? And why are you defending him?"

"Did he stay with you?" Nick repeated. "With his family?"

She stared at him, then said reluctantly, "Yes."

"Not all parents do. That's all I'm saying."

She pulled her hand away and buried her face in her hands while she rocked back and forth. "She forgave him. How could my mother forgive him?"

"Because she didn't want to break up your family. And maybe she still loved him. Casey, he made a mistake that a lot of other people have made. If he wasn't your father, you wouldn't be condemning him categorically."

She was glaring at him as if she wanted to spit-roast him over an open fire. She wanted him to agree that her father deserved castration, not understanding or reasonable explanations of his behavior.

Exasperated, he sighed. "Look, I'm not saying he

didn't do something wrong. But it's not going to help you to hold on to this anger. Especially when underneath it you're still grieving.''

''So I'm just supposed to forget what he did? That's going to be a little hard, since my new *sister* is named in the will. She'll be coming to Bellefontaine sometime after the funeral.''

Nick frowned. No surprise, he guessed, but still not good news for Casey and Jackson. ''You don't have to think about that now. You're having a hard enough time with your parents' deaths. Anyone would. Can't you let it go, at least for now?''

''I don't know.'' She turned her head away and spoke so softly he had a hard time hearing her. ''It's easier to be angry. If I'm angry I don't think as much about the really bad part.'' She looked at him. ''I don't want to think about never seeing them again.''

''I know.''

Her eyes filled with tears, of sorrow this time. He took her into his arms, put her head on his shoulder and listened to her cry.

And later, when she'd stopped crying, he took her upstairs and held her through the long night.

CHAPTER EIGHTEEN

CASEY SLEPT in Nick's bed, in his arms. She talked, she cried. She raged and despaired. And through it all, he listened and comforted her, lending her his strength.

She'd been too exhausted, had needed him too much to even question why he was there. But the next morning, as she lay listening to his even breathing, she knew last night had been about far more than simply helping a friend. Nick loved her, and nothing he said, certainly no fixation with his past, was going to convince her that they were better off apart.

She got up and showered, feeling marginally better, even though her eyes were still gritty and swollen. When she went downstairs to the tiny kitchen, she found Nick having coffee and talking on the phone.

"Yeah, she just walked in," he said, handing her the receiver. "It's Remy Boucherand. He's got some news for you," he said and poured coffee into a mug for her. Then he left the room to take a shower.

Remy had dropped by Bellefontaine the day before to offer the family his sympathy, so Casey wasn't quite sure why he'd tracked her down to Nick's. After the bad news that had been dogging her lately, she was afraid to ask. "Hi, Remy."

"Hi, Casey. Sorry to bother you, but something important has come up. I'm afraid it can't wait."

"That's okay. What is it?"

"We have Harold Broderick in custody. Picked him up last night in a bar brawl."

Broderick. God, that seemed like a lifetime ago, and it had only been a matter of days since he'd tried to kill her. She touched her neck reflectively. "Good. I'm glad you found him."

"Casey, I realize it's a bad time for you, but I need you to come identify him as your attacker. I'd like Nick to come, too. And your aunt Esme."

"Aunt Esme? Why?" She took a sip of coffee and tried to clear her mind, unsuccessfully.

"The fire at Bellefontaine. Remember your aunt said a dark-haired man shoved her down? It's possible Broderick is that man."

"You think Broderick set the fire? No one seemed to think much of her statement at the time. You said it was too unclear to be of much use."

"It was unclear. And then this joker attacked you. The crimes might be related. We have evidence that could tie Broderick to the arson, but I need reason-

able cause to go farther. I know it's a lot to ask, especially right now, but do you think you can come down here to the station and bring your aunt with you? I've already talked to Nick, and he said he'd come with you.''

"I'll try." She sighed and ran a hand through her hair. ''Aunt Esme's having a rough time.'' Remy made a sound of sympathy. ''We—'' She hesitated, not wanting to expose all of the Fontaine's dirty laundry, but if Noelani Hana came to Bellefontaine, everyone would know soon enough who she was and what she was doing there. Besides, Remy was a friend. ''We had some other news yesterday that's upset her. Something in addition to my parents' deaths.''

''I'm sorry,'' he said, sounding concerned. ''Anything you want to talk about?''

''Not really.''

''Will I hear about it later?''

''Probably.'' Undoubtedly. ''I'd better tell you. Duke has an illegitimate daughter.''

Remy was silent for several seconds. Then he whistled. ''Wow. Guess that was a shocker for all of you.''

''Understatement of the year,'' she agreed. ''Jackson and I had no idea. Not even Aunt Esme knew about it.''

''I don't know what to say, Casey.''

"That's because there's not much *to* say. I just wanted you to know before the gossip starts to spread. We'll be down there as soon as we can."

A COUPLE OF HOURS LATER Casey and Nick had both positively identified Harold Broderick in a lineup. Esme had been less sure, but Remy seemed to think he had probable cause to proceed with his case. They left the station with Remy's promise to call once anything definite happened.

Casey had asked Nick to drive them in her mother's Cadillac. As they neared the house, she shot a glance at her aunt, seated rigidly in the front seat. Esme hadn't even complained about Nick.

Casey was really worried about her aunt. Although only in her early sixties, lately she looked fifteen years older, and broken. On top of not complaining, she had even allowed Nick to help her in and out of the car, leaning on him on the way into the station, as if she'd never said a bad word about him. Casey decided even her aunt's scathing commentaries on Casey's behavior would be preferable to the way she was behaving now.

But Esme had been devastated, just as they all had. One thing after another had happened to shatter their peace. It would be foolish to expect her to bounce back right away. Casey sure hadn't, and she was a lot younger than Esme.

Nick pulled into the garage. Casey got out and waited while Nick helped Esme out of the car. She took her aunt's other arm, shocked at how frail it felt.

"Your parents are coming home today," Esme said as they entered the house through the back porch door.

Casey exchanged a startled glance with Nick. "Aunt Esme, Maman and Duke…they're gone."

"I'm well aware of that," Esme said acerbically, sounding more like herself. "I'm neither senile nor stupid."

Casey closed her eyes. *Oh God, she's talking about their bodies.*

"Jackson set the funeral for the day after tomorrow," Esme continued. She sat down at the breakfast table they'd moved onto the porch for the duration of the renovation, and frowned at Casey. "We should make some calls in case not everyone sees the paper. Your friend Viv has offered to help."

The very last thing Casey wanted to do was to make those calls, but she couldn't leave the burden on her aunt's shoulders. She nodded, not speaking.

"If you'll give me a list, I'll be glad to make some of the calls for you, too," Nick said.

"Thank you. That's very thoughtful of you." Esme gazed at Nick before adding, "Perhaps I was

wrong about you. You've been very kind. Both to me and my niece.''

Nick smiled and shook his head. ''No, Miss Esme, you were exactly right. I'm still that no-account gambler you thought I was when we first met.'' To Casey he said, ''I have to go to the boat but I'll be back soon.''

''I'll walk you out,'' she said, responding to his signal.

''Make sure your aunt eats something,'' he said when they got outside. ''She looks like she's going to keel over if she doesn't.''

''I'll have Betty fix something quick. Sandwiches, maybe.'' She could use food, too. Her stomach had been so jumpy she'd hardly eaten since the eggs Betty had fixed her at lunch the day before.

''And you eat, as well,'' he added, reading her mind. ''It won't help anyone if both you and your aunt pass out.''

''I will. Nick, thank you. Not just for today, but for last night. I didn't want to be alone.''

He shrugged and glanced away. ''You could have stayed with your family.''

''I didn't want them. I wanted you.''

He looked at her and she was startled to see the torment in his eyes. ''Casey, don't read any more into this—into my being here—than it is. It will just make matters that much worse in the end.''

"I know that's what you say." She put her arms around his neck and kissed him, until he slowly, reluctantly kissed her back. "But it's not how you feel, is it, Nick?"

"I have to go," he said, and left her abruptly.

In spite of everything, her heart felt a bit lighter. Nick cared, no matter what he said.

When she went back inside, to her surprise, Esme was still sitting at the table.

"That young man is in love with you."

"I know."

"But does he know it?"

Casey nodded. "Yes. He's just having trouble admitting we could last. I intend to change his mind."

"I'm sure you'll manage," Esme said dryly. "You are a Fontaine."

THE NEXT FEW DAYS, including the funeral itself, passed in a blur for Casey. The only mercy was that getting ready for the influx of mourners, and those people who would stay overnight after the services, took up so much of her attention that she didn't have much time left over to dwell on her newest relation and what was going to happen to Bellefontaine.

To Casey's surprise, the funeral brought her a measure of peace. While she hadn't been able to totally forgive her father for what she still thought of as his betrayal, she was able to mourn for both

her parents sincerely. And seeing the number of people who'd come—from friends, acquaintances and employees to their many relations—brought her comfort, as well. Duke and Angelique had mattered to a great many people and would be sorely missed.

She spent the nights with Nick, and they were both very careful not to mention when he planned to leave or how she planned to deal with it when he did. They didn't make love, but Casey stayed every night in his bed and in his arms. She wondered how he could be so blind to the commitment he'd made to her.

Casey went back to work the day after the funeral. Not only did Len need help with the harvest—he'd been working on his own for days—but she needed to do something worthwhile. Something that might take her mind off Nick and her new sister. Besides, it made her feel closer to her father, doing something he would have approved of. He wouldn't want them to neglect Bellefontaine.

A couple of days later, while she was out in the fields, she got a call from Jackson on her cell phone.

"Remy Boucherand is coming over. He wants to see you, me and Aunt Esme."

"Is it about Broderick?"

"Yes. He'll be here in about half an hour."

"All right, see you then."

They met with Remy in the billiards room, the

same room in which they'd discussed the fire with the Fire Captain, the first night she'd seen Nick. She sighed and tried to focus on the matter at hand.

Remy waited until they were all seated and then began. "It looks like Harold Broderick is responsible for a lot of your problems. We had him cold on the vandalism and assault charges, since both Nick and Casey identified him. We were also able to match a fingerprint we found in the kitchen to his. When he realized we had him on that one, he confessed to setting the fire, as well. He's also confessed to a third crime."

"The stolen harvester?" Jackson asked.

Remy nodded. "That's right. He arranged to have it stolen, and the story he gave checks out."

"But why did he confess?" Casey asked. "Did you have any proof?"

Remy smiled at her. "No, we didn't even have a lead on it. Broderick wanted to make a deal. Here's the interesting part. Broderick claims he acted under orders. Says he committed all three crimes at someone else's instigation."

They all exchanged glances. Casey said, "Someone paid him to do all those things? Why?"

"That, he doesn't know. Unfortunately, he also has no idea who his employer was." He rubbed his jaw and sighed. "I've got to tell you, we don't have a lot of faith in the man's confession."

"Why not?" Esme asked. "Why would he confess to another crime if he didn't do it?"

"Oh, we think he did it. We just don't believe someone paid him. He can't identify the man. Claims he was paid cash, that the money was dropped off in a locker at the bus station. And here's the real kicker—he's since lost the money. Says he gambled it away."

"Obviously you haven't been able to verify that fact," Jackson said. "So you think Broderick was operating on his own and he made up the conspiracy to get himself off the hook."

Remy nodded. "It's the most logical explanation. Broderick's really got it in for your sister. He's irrational where she's concerned. When she fired him, it sent him off the deep end. Between you and me, he didn't have far to go."

"What was I supposed to do?" Casey asked, annoyed. "The man came to work drunk. Twice. Any rational person would have fired him."

"I'm not arguing, *chère,*" Remy said soothingly. "Just explaining his motivation."

"Any hope of getting our harvester back?" Casey asked, thinking of the increase in their insurance rates. If they recovered the harvester, that might lessen the blow.

"Sorry, *chère,*" Remy said, and got up. "Virtually none. That machine could be anywhere in Mex-

ico by now. We'll do what we can with what he told us, but don't get your hopes up.''

It looked like she'd have to be satisfied with having Harold Broderick behind bars. Besides, she had other things to think about now. Like Nick and her.

She'd decided that she wasn't giving up Nick without a fight. And she knew she had to act quickly, since she was sure he'd be leaving soon. In a perfect world, she could have taken her time, but her world had been anything but perfect lately.

Exactly how she intended to accomplish her goal, she wasn't sure. She thought she might have an idea to get them started in the right direction, though.

She was going to seduce Nick, and take it from there.

CHAPTER NINETEEN

NICK WENT TO CASEY'S that evening after he finished up at the casino. She'd called earlier and asked
him if he would come over, and he hadn't been able
to think of a good reason not to. Except that the
cottage held too many memories of their making
love.

But he didn't think she wanted to hear that, so he
told her he would come by. And now that he'd arrived, he had regrets. It had been hard enough sleeping with Casey, holding her in his arms every night,
but never making love to her. Only that morning
he'd woken up with a hard-on the size of Texas.
He'd wanted to kiss her awake and make long, slow
love to her for hours, then start all over again. Instead, he'd rolled out of bed and headed straight into
a cold shower.

So he wouldn't spend the night with her again.
Because if he stayed the night, even one more night,
he would lose control and they'd make love. And
that would be a mistake for both of them.

Casey needed to get accustomed to his absence.

He'd been there for her after her parents died, and he didn't regret that for a minute. He couldn't have left her when she was so vulnerable, when she'd needed him so much. But she couldn't continue to lean on him—not when he'd be leaving soon. In truth, he could leave next week if he wanted to.

He used the key she'd given him and stepped inside, halting on the threshold in shock. A score of candles lit the room, casting a romantic glow. The house smelled incredible—expensive, exotic, like a hothouse or tropical garden. It looked like one, too, with flowers of all varieties in vases on every flat surface. He was surprised rose petals weren't leading the way to her.

His eyes lifted to meet Casey's. She sat on the couch wearing an extremely sheer nightgown the color of her eyes. For an intense moment he simply stared at her. Finally, his brain began to function again. *Oh, shit, I'm dead meat now,* was all he could think.

Casey laughed softly. "You look absolutely panic-stricken, Nick. Surely a romantic setting isn't enough to put that expression in your eyes."

No possible way could he resist her in this mood. But he had to try. "What the hell are you doing?" he asked, surprised he could speak without stuttering.

She didn't respond, but smiled and poured wine

into two crystal glasses. "You're an intelligent man," she said, picking up a glass and rising. "I'm sure you'll figure it out. Now shut the door, Nick, you're letting all the cool air out. And come have a glass of wine."

He closed the door with a bang and walked toward her. He tried his best to keep his eyes on her face, but with all the smooth, glowing skin exposed by the nightgown, he didn't stand a chance. His eyes were riveted, as he was sure she'd intended, on the very tempting swells of her breasts. He took the glass she handed him and gulped down some wine.

"Nice," he said, and picked up the bottle. "I wasn't aware you knew wine." Excellent vintage. Pricey as hell. Or it had been the last time he'd had it, in Monte Carlo. He wondered what a bottle went for nowadays. It appeared Casey was pulling out all the stops.

"I don't know a thing about wine." She grinned. "I got it from the wine cellar at Bellefontaine. What I do know is where they keep the good stuff."

"So, what's the occasion?" Two more minutes and he'd be sweating. No, begging. He hadn't seen her smile like that in far too long.

"Nothing. Just…to us." She picked up her glass and touched it to his. She tasted hers, grimaced and set it down on the coffee table. "Are you sure the wine isn't sour? It tastes funny to me."

"No, it's great." He took another sip to prove it. Smooth and rich, just like her skin. He set the glass on the coffee table. "I hate to ruin your plans, but I think we can cut to the chase. This isn't going to happen."

"What isn't going to happen, Nick? Our making love?"

She tilted her head and smiled, a sultry, sexy smile that made him want to say to hell with his scruples.

"Why not?" she asked.

He hardened his heart, and his voice. "It's over between us, Casey. These past few days you needed a friend. That's all I've been."

She moved closer to him and put her arms around his neck. She kissed his jaw, a string of tiny nips that were as arousing as anything he'd ever experienced. He felt sweat pop out on his forehead and gritted his teeth.

"Liar," she said softly in his ear. "I've been sleeping next to you, remember? You still want me."

Want her? More than he'd ever wanted anyone in his life. "I'm leaving town next week," he said desperately, as her fingers unbuttoned his shirt and her mouth—Lord, that mouth—followed her fingers, skimming his chest with heated kisses. He was mes-

merized by Casey, swamped in her scent, the feel of her skin, soft and warm against his.

"Really?" She shoved his shirt down his arms, her eyes alive with wicked laughter. "Sudden decision, isn't it?" She rubbed her breasts, covered only by a thin layer of silk, against his bare chest.

He couldn't stop a groan. Couldn't stop his arms from going around her, his hands from clamping on her hips, holding her tight against him. "You're killing me," he said, and crushed his mouth to hers.

"That's the idea," she whispered, when he let her up for air.

He knew it was wrong. Hell, he knew it was the biggest mistake he'd ever made. But there was no way in hell he was leaving her house without making love to her. Without putting his mouth on every inch of her luscious skin, and having her mouth on him. Without being inside her and knowing that last taste of heaven.

"I can't fight you any longer," he said, and kissed her again.

By the time they reached her bedroom they were both naked. He barely managed to put on a condom before he parted her thighs. Her back arched, and her hips lifted to meet his. He'd wanted to make it last, but Casey was as frantic as he was, her hands and her mouth urging him to completion as her body tightened around him.

"Too fast," he said, trying to slow down. He kissed her mouth, mating his tongue with hers.

"Just right," she whispered when his mouth moved to her throat to taste her.

Her eyes glazed, and he felt her convulse around him. As her muscles contracted, he drove into her again and again, and spilled deep inside her.

"Nick? Are you awake?"

They were lying in bed, and she had her head on his shoulder and was tracing circles on his chest with her fingers. It was later, much later, after they'd made love again. Nick had never felt as content as he did at that moment. But the feeling couldn't last…could it?

"I'm awake."

"Stay with me."

He looked down at her and smiled. "I'm not going anywhere." Not tonight, anyway.

"No. I mean, stay for good. Live with me, here at the cottage."

Damn it, hadn't he known it was a mistake to make love with her? Now she was dreaming about happily ever after, and if Nick knew one thing, it was that he wasn't fated for happily ever after.

"I can't. I told you that before and nothing's changed." He got out of bed and went looking for his pants. He found them in the hall, pulled them on

and went into the kitchen to pour himself a glass of water. He considered drinking the wine, since he knew damn well that Casey wouldn't let this subject drop.

She didn't. A few minutes later, she came into the room wearing a soft terry-cloth robe. She didn't look particularly upset, though she did seem a little exasperated. She sat on the couch and watched him finish the glass of water.

"You can't keep running, Nick. Sooner or later you're going to have to face it."

He shoved his hands through his hair and glared at her. "Face what?"

"Your past. Or whatever it is about your past you can't deal with."

"You're wrong. I've been avoiding it for nearly thirty years now. I see no reason to change."

She frowned. "Well, beyond the obvious reason that you're never going to have a permanent relationship until you deal with it, I guess that's true."

He walked into the living room and sat on the couch, as far away from Casey as he could get. He picked up the glass of wine and drank it, then poured more into his glass. He started to fill hers, but she covered the glass with her hand.

"You didn't tell me all of it, did you?"

He shook his head. "There was no reason to. Not then, or now."

"Tell me."

"I don't talk about it. Ever. There's no point."

"I think you're wrong." She put her hand on his arm and rubbed it up and down, comfortingly. "What are you hiding from?"

He set the wineglass down with a *bang*. "Damn it, I'm not hiding from anything. It was a miserable time in my life. Why should I talk about it? Besides, it was years ago."

She didn't lose her temper. She remained maddeningly calm. "You said you went into the orphanage when you were seven. Tell me about the time before that."

He turned his head and glared at her again. Why the hell couldn't she just leave it alone? Why did she have to push him to remember something he'd buried for the better part of three decades? Something that should stay buried. Something too shameful to even think about, much less talk about.

"You're not getting off my back until I talk, are you?"

"No." She smiled ruefully. "I want to understand. I want to help you."

"I can't understand it—why should you?" He focused on a vase of flowers. Tiger lilies. Fiery splashes of orange and red. Beautiful and exotic. He couldn't remember the first time he'd seen flowers. There sure as hell hadn't been any vases sitting

around his parents' apartment or any beds of plants surrounding the desolate buildings of inner-city Dallas. Not even a damn daisy or wildflower had dared showed itself in that neighborhood.

Get it over with, he told himself. *Just do it.* "We lived in Texas. Dallas, Texas. At least, I think we did. That's where the orphanage was. Before the orphanage…it was bad. Hell, I was seven years old. I don't remember much except screaming, yelling and hitting. My old man wasn't great, but my mother was worse."

"Why? What did she do?"

It was coming back to him. He had thought he'd forgotten, but he hadn't. "As long as I stayed out of my old man's way I was okay. He'd slap me around some if I bugged him, but nothing too bad. I don't think he broke any bones." He laughed bitterly. Casey rubbed his arm again, but stayed silent. "But she…my mother hated me. Hated that she'd had me. She was always telling my old man she wouldn't have stuck around if it hadn't been for me. And instead of blaming him for getting her pregnant, she blamed me. Just for being there."

"Nick, you were a child. It wasn't your fault."

"I know that." He looked at her then, at the concern in her eyes. He tapped a finger to his temple. "I know it here."

He was quiet for a moment, until Casey asked, "When did they leave you at the orphanage?"

"I was seven. That's all I remember." But it wasn't. He swallowed hard and his throat closed up. He remembered the rest of it, too damn clearly.

"Nick, I don't think that's true."

"Goddamn it, I told you I didn't want to talk about it. Why can't you let it go?" He chugged the rest of his wine.

"Your parents didn't take you to the orphanage, did they?"

He closed his eyes. "No," he said, his voice very low.

"What happened?"

He looked at her, at those green eyes, so wide and trusting. So sad, as if she could feel his pain. But he didn't ever want Casey to have to deal with that. It was too ugly.

"They—oh, shit—*she* locked me in a closet. She'd been drinking, and I was hungry. We didn't have any food. That was nothing new. She got sick of me whining about being hungry, so she locked me in the closet."

"And?" she asked softly.

He struggled, trying to pretend the rush of memories didn't hurt almost as much now as they had then. "And she left me there. She just took off. My old man had split a week or so before, and she de-

cided she didn't want to bother with me anymore. She cut her losses—that was me—and ran.''

She was staring at him, her eyes filling with tears.

"I told you it wasn't pretty.''

"I can't imagine anyone doing that to a child.''

"Yeah, well, believe it. I guess she had a change of heart or something. She called one of the neighbors and told them where I was. The police came and took me away. I ended up at the orphanage. End of story.'' He slumped back, drained from telling her.

"How long were you there? In the closet?''

He shrugged. "A day or two. I don't really know. Couldn't have been too long, since I didn't have any food or water. Might have been just a few hours. It pretty much seems like for-goddamn-ever when you're locked inside a closet.''

"Did you get any counseling?''

He shot her a disbelieving glance. "Yeah, sure. Tons of it.''

Her eyes were soft, compassionate. "So this is why you never stay in one place? Because you don't trust anyone to be there for you?''

He hadn't really thought about it like that. Maybe she was right. "Would you?''

"I...guess I wouldn't. But you're letting it ruin your life.''

"Don't you get it?'' he asked her savagely. "My

own mother didn't want me. She left me in a closet rather than take care of me. How can I expect someone else to love me when my own parents, my own mother, hated my guts?"

"I love you."

"You think you do." He would just disappoint her.

"I know I do. And you love me, too."

"Didn't you hear a word I said?"

"Every word. I understand you're scared. But Nick, nothing's ever going to be as bad as what you've already been through."

"You're wrong. Losing you would be worse."

"So you're not even going to give us a chance? Take a gamble, Nick. You've spent your whole career betting on risky propositions. Why not take this chance…on us?"

He shook his head. "The stakes are too high."

"No, they're not. You're worth it, Nick. We're worth it."

"Casey, I can't."

"You mean, you won't."

"No, I won't."

He'd already survived losing everything once. He couldn't risk it again. Not for her sake…and not for his.

CHAPTER TWENTY

"YOUR MIND IS MADE UP, isn't it?" she said. "You're leaving, and nothing I say is going to change your mind."

He nodded, not trusting himself to speak. He expected her to argue. Or to kick him out. But Casey did neither of those things. She just looked at him, her eyes deep pools of compassion, then took his hand and led him back to her bedroom, to her bed. And she made love to him.

Nick didn't sleep that night, but Casey did. He watched her while she slept in his arms as she'd done before, but this time there was a difference. This time they both knew it would be the last.

Finally, just before dawn, he got up and went into the other room. He sat on the couch, as he had the first night he'd spent with her. He hadn't known then that he was going to fall in love with Casey and that his world would never be the same.

He had to leave. If he stayed, he'd only let Casey down. If he stayed, the end would be that much harder.

Except he didn't see how anything could be harder than leaving Casey, knowing that she loved him. *"You're worth it,"* she'd told him. And he knew she meant it. He'd never in his life felt as if he were worthwhile to another person. In business, sure. But not emotionally.

Casey had put herself on the line for him. She'd risked everything to keep him, making herself vulnerable by asking him to stay. She hadn't let pride stand in her way. It couldn't have been easy for her, especially not since she'd had her heart trampled by another man who hadn't been worthy of her love.

And how had Nick responded when she'd offered him her love? He'd thrown it right back in her face. Because he was too afraid of failure to even risk trying. Some gambler he was.

What did he expect to gain by leaving her? Going away wouldn't change his feelings. He'd fallen in love with Casey. He would only be punishing both of them.

If he stayed… He could have a home. A family. Best of all, he could have Casey, as his wife. Sure, there was no guarantee that everything would work out, that their marriage would last. But Casey had been willing to try. Because she thought the rewards were worth the risk.

Now, so did he.

THEY HADN'T TALKED ANY MORE the night before, or at least, not about Nick's past or their future.

Casey had done all she could. She couldn't force Nick to take a chance on them, just as she couldn't force the bad memories from his mind. She could only love him and hope that he would decide he wanted to face a future with her instead of staying mired in the past.

So while they didn't talk, they made love several times. Casey suspected he didn't sleep at all, but she dozed off around dawn, waking, when the sun was high, to find Nick long gone. She stretched, turned her head on the pillow and saw a folded note. She hesitated before picking it up, unsure whether she wanted to read it.

I love you.

That was all it said. But those three words were enough to give her hope.

Nick had never before voluntarily admitted he loved her. Smiling, she tucked the note next to her heart, then a moment later realized how late it was and shot out of bed. Len was going to kill her if she didn't get to work.

Her stomach rolled and she made a dash for the bathroom. Several wretched moments later, she finished heaving, thankful Nick hadn't been around to witness her throwing up. She washed her face and rinsed out her mouth, unable to ignore the signs any longer. She had to admit the truth—to herself, at least.

She'd thought it had all been stress related. Her symptoms had coincided with everything that had been happening. Her parents' death had only added to the stress, so she hadn't been surprised that her cycle was off and her stomach wasn't behaving normally. Besides, she'd told herself, it was too soon to know anything for certain.

But this wasn't stress. She was pregnant. Somehow, despite using birth control, she'd gotten pregnant. And there was no way she intended to tell Nick as a means to force him to stay with her. Casey didn't know exactly what she planned to do, but she wanted Nick to stay with her because he wanted her. Not because they were going to have a child together.

She returned to the cottage later that evening, dog tired and filthy dirty. And starving. After grabbing an apple to tide her over, she decided to take a bath instead of a shower. She added bubble bath, climbed in and promptly fell asleep.

She woke to find Nick kneeling beside the tub, stroking a single red rose down her cheek. She couldn't have been asleep too long, because the water was still warm and there were still bubbles.

"Wake up, Sleeping Beauty."

Casey blinked at him. "If I'm Sleeping Beauty, does that make you the Prince?"

He laughed and leaned down to kiss her. A soft, tender, drawn-out kiss that made her head spin. He got to his feet and picked up the towel she'd set aside, laying the rose on the sink. "Come on, I've brought dinner. I had the chef at the White Gold prepare something special. Tournedos Diablo on a bed of wild rice."

"Sounds wonderful," she said, letting him wrap her in the fluffy towel. "I'm starved."

"Me, too." He dropped a kiss on her neck and handed her the rose. "I'll meet you in the kitchen."

She started to get dressed, then decided she was too hungry and grabbed a robe. A royal-blue silky one her grandmother had brought from Paris. She walked into the kitchen and stopped, touched by the scene he'd set. A vase of roses sat on the table, along with a brace of lit candles. Somehow he'd unearthed her grandmother's good china and crystal and set the table with them.

"It smells wonderful." He started to fill her wine-glass, but she shook her head. "I'll just have water. Alcohol hasn't been agreeing with me lately." And she knew why, though she hoped he didn't.

They ate in silence, for the most part. He seemed in a strange mood, but she was just grateful he hadn't left yet, so she didn't question him. She finished and laid her fork aside. "I feel human again.

Thanks. What did you do today, besides have your chef create this?'' She gestured at the food.

"I've been busy. Moreau is finally taking over the White Gold. Next week. I'd had my doubts about him working out, but I found out he's been having marital problems. Supposedly they're solved now, so he should be able to take over.''

Which meant he'd be leaving, after all. Her hopes died. "Really? So soon?''

He nodded, then got up and reached out to her. "Let's go in the other room. I'll clean this up later.''

"No, I'll clean it up. You brought the food, it's only fair I clean up.''

"Fine, but I want to talk to you first.''

Her heart sank, but she followed him into the other room, trying desperately not to think about what he was going to say. In fact, she was trying so hard she didn't hear what he actually said.

"I'm sorry…what did you say?''

He laughed and handed her a rose. "So much for my declaration of undying love.''

"Is that what you said?''

"I asked you if you knew what a single red rose in full bloom means.''

She glanced at the flower, then at him. "No idea.''

"It means, I love you.''

She just looked at him. "But not enough to stay."

He ignored that. "Do you know what else I did today? Besides getting the White Gold ready for the transfer."

She shook her head, wondering if he really meant to torture her, or if he was just dense.

He continued. "I made a couple of transactions today. Interesting transactions."

"That's nice." She wanted to slap him upside the head, but she restrained herself.

"I hope you'll think so. Don't you want to know what they are?"

She gave him a dirty look. "Oh, do tell."

"I arranged to buy a shipyard. In St. Louis. They make floating casinos. I've bought boats from them in the past, so I know something about their operation."

"So you're going to St. Louis," she said flatly. *"Bon voyage."*

He didn't respond to that, either, except to give her the same maddening smile. "I made another purchase, too. A riverboat casino. It's run-down, needs a lot of work. They've lost a lot of customers. It's been badly mismanaged."

She clenched her jaw, and her fist, quelling the urge to deck him. "Where is it? New Orleans? St. Louis? Or have you decided to go back to Europe?"

"It's right here in Baton Rouge, Casey."

She blinked at him, sure she hadn't heard him right. "Here? Why?" she whispered. She looked into his eyes and her heart began to pound.

He took one of her hands and brought it to his mouth. Kissed it, then held it. "I thought it was time to take that gamble."

"Wh-what gamble?"

"The one you talked about. To gamble on us. I didn't sleep much last night, so it gave me a lot of time to think. To think about being without you and what I was going to feel like when I realized I'd lost you, all because I was too afraid to take a chance. When I was a kid, I didn't have a choice. But I do now."

"You're staying?" She was having a hard time breathing. "Just like that, you've changed your mind?"

He smiled. "It wasn't exactly 'just like that.' I thought about what you said, and I knew you were right. My past shaped me, and I can't change that. But I don't have to repeat the behavior. I don't have to choose that kind of life." He took her face in his hands, leaned forward and kissed her. Long and sweet.

"I thought about never seeing you again, or holding you, or loving you, and I couldn't do it. I didn't want to do it. I could live without you, Casey. And

you could live without me. But I think we'll be a lot happier with each other.''

"So are you going to move in with me?"

He shook his head, but he was smiling. "I don't want to live with you. I want to marry you. I want the whole enchilada. Marriage, home, kids."

He reached into his pocket and pulled out a jewelers box. "It's not traditional," he said, and opened it. A gorgeous band of emeralds and diamonds sat inside on a bed of velvet. "The emeralds remind me of your eyes."

"It's beautiful."

"Will you marry me, Casey?"

"Yes." She had to whisper the word because her heart was so full she thought it would burst. She held out her hand, and he slipped the ring on, then kissed her. Soon she wasn't wearing anything but his ring, and he was showing her just exactly how much he loved her.

"Nick," she said later, lying in bed with him. "Do you think I'm terrible to be happy? Now, I mean. With Maman and Duke— It wasn't very long ago that…" She didn't want to say the words.

He held her close and stroked his hand over her hair comfortingly. "From everything you've said about your parents, I think they'd want you to be happy. I don't think they'd want you feeling guilty."

"They wouldn't. I know they wouldn't. I

just…miss them. I wish I could have shared this with them.''

''I wish you could have, too.''

Casey decided she should tell Nick about her suspicions. ''Did you mean it when you said you wanted kids?''

He smiled at her and kissed her nose. ''Yeah, I do. Don't you?''

She breathed a huge sigh of relief. She'd thought that would be his answer, but it was nice to know for certain. ''Very much. Which is a good thing.''

He stared at her, then grinned, ''Are you trying to tell me something?''

She couldn't stop smiling, either. ''I haven't taken a test yet, but I think I'm pregnant.''

''You're going to have a baby?'' He put his hand on her stomach. ''Our baby?''

She nodded. ''I'm almost sure. Do you mind? Especially that it's so soon?''

He shook his head. ''No, I'm happy about it. I'm just surprised.''

''I know. It was a surprise to me, too. I thought it was stress at first.''

''Would you have told me? If I'd left?''

He looked troubled, and she couldn't blame him. ''Yes. I would never have kept that from you. But I wanted you to stay for me, not because you felt you had to because of the baby.''

He kissed her, then drew back and smiled. "You know what this means, don't you?"

"That we're going to be parents?"

"That, too. But it means we don't have to wait. We can get married soon."

"You're right." She smiled and kissed him. "How does next weekend sound to you?"

"Perfect."

EPILOGUE

"WHAT'S WRONG, Mrs. Devlin, can't you sleep?" Nick slipped his arms around Casey from behind and nuzzled her neck. She was standing out on the balcony of their hotel room in the French Quarter of New Orleans.

She tilted her head. "I was just thinking. About my parents. I wish they could have been at the wedding."

"I know. I'm sorry I never met them." They'd held the wedding at the church, since Casey hadn't wanted to have it at Bellefontaine so soon after the funeral.

"Duke would have liked you. So would Maman."

He laughed. "Your aunt Esme sure doesn't. I half expected her to protest during the wedding." It had been a very small wedding, with only the family, Luc and Viv Renault, Adam Ross and Remy Boucherand in attendance.

"Oh, there was never any fear of that." She dimpled and looked over her shoulder. "Aunt Esme

would never cause a scene in a church. Besides, she's decided you're not so bad. She doesn't say it, but she's looking forward to another grandniece or nephew.''

He put his hands on her still-flat stomach. ''It's hard for me to believe we have a baby in here.'' Hard for him to imagine being a father. But he knew one thing. He and Casey were going to love this child, and each other.

''You'd believe it if you had my morning sickness.'' They both laughed. She rubbed her cheek on his shoulder. ''The wedding was beautiful, wasn't it? I don't think I've ever seen Megan so excited.'' She sighed, but he didn't think she sounded content.

''What's wrong?''

''You know me already, don't you?''

He turned her around. ''Are you regretting we got married so soon?''

She put her hand on his cheek. ''No, of course not. What about you? Do you have any regrets?''

''Not a single one,'' he said, turning his face into her palm and kissing it.

''I'm glad we didn't have to wait. Having you with me is going to help when…when Noelani Hana comes to town.''

''You heard something?''

She nodded. ''Jackson called this morning while you were in the shower. She's coming a few days

after we get back from our honeymoon. Shelbourne is anxious to read the will. I'm dreading it. We have no idea how Duke left things, not anymore.''

Nick frowned. ''I knew we shouldn't have told Jackson where we were going. Couldn't he have waited to tell you when we got home?''

''I think he wanted to give me time to prepare myself. He didn't want to hit me with the news the minute we got home.''

''Stop worrying so much. Maybe she won't be as bad as you think.''

''Maybe.''

She still looked doubtful, so Nick decided a little distraction was in order. He slipped his hands inside her robe and cupped her breasts, rubbing his thumbs across her nipples.

Her eyes clouded and she gave a tiny moan. ''What are you doing?''

''I'm about to make love to you. Much more fun than worrying about things we can't do anything about, don't you think?''

''Definitely. I love you, Nick.''

''I love you, too,'' he said, and kissed her tenderly.

Then he took her inside and made love to her until neither one of them was worried about anything.

*　*　*　*　*

Turn the page to read an excerpt from
THE SECRET DAUGHTER
by Roz Denny Fox,
the second book in the
RAISING CANE *trilogy.*

CHAPTER ONE

"NOELANI, IT GRIEVES ME greatly, but I have the task of telling you that Duke Fontaine and his wife, Angelique, died in a plane crash." Bruce Shiller pushed the letter toward her. "This lawyer, Shelburne Prescott, says you're named in your father's will, along with Cassandra and Jackson Fontaine. They, of course, live at Bellefontaine. Duke's plantation...on the mainland," he clarified, as Noelani stared at the letter without touching it.

"He had other kids? Well, if they're named Fontaine, I guess they're legitimate."

"Noelani!"

She crumpled the page and threw it back across the desk. "What am I supposed to feel, Bruce? Sorrow...for someone who didn't give a damn about me? I'd never even *met* the man!"

"You should have gone there after your mother died."

"I didn't need him. I had Grandmother. And I had you." She shook her head. "Did he come to her funeral or even send flowers? I know you

notified him.'' Furious now, as she always was when she thought about the man her mother had thrown away her life for, Noelani twisted a lock of hair. The auburn streaks and her five-foot-six-inch height were attributes she'd probably inherited from Duke Fontaine. If Noelani felt curious about anything, it was what traits she shared with half siblings she hadn't known existed until this minute.

"Duke cared enough to name you in his will. His sugarcane operation makes mine look like small potatoes, kid. You think it's not obvious, but you're practically killing yourself in my mill, trying to achieve what Duke's children have by birthright.''

The initial shock of Bruce's news had begun to fade. In purely mercenary terms, Noelani considered what she could do with a windfall of cash. Do here—at Shiller's, she hastily corrected. Except... wasn't there always a catch when it came to money? In this case, she'd have to admit she was Duke Fontaine's bastard.

She eyed the balled letter belligerently. "I can't imagine that Duke's legitimate kids want me appearing on the scene to muck up their lives. How old are they?''

"Cassandra is thirty or thirty-one. Jackson's a little younger. Nearer your age. Girl, you owe it to yourself to at least go see what this inheritance is

all about. Who knows?—you may like Louisiana and Duke's family well enough to stay.''

"Forget it. I don't need Duke Fontaine's guilt money. I don't need anything from him. I never have!''

"Noelani, do this for your mother. Anela never stopped loving him. Anyway, aren't you curious? Over the years you've asked questions about your biological dad. This is your chance to get answers.''

Vaulting from her chair, Noelani stalked to the door, angry tears glistening in her eyes. ''That's dirty pool,'' she finally said in a hard-edged voice. "Okay, I'll go. But the minute his affairs are settled, I'm on the next plane back to Maui.''

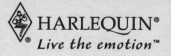

If you enjoyed what you just read,
then we've got an offer you can't resist!

Take 2 bestselling
love stories FREE!
Plus get a FREE surprise gift!

///////////////////////////////////

Clip this page and mail it to Harlequin Reader Service®

IN U.S.A.	IN CANADA
3010 Walden Ave.	P.O. Box 609
P.O. Box 1867	Fort Erie, Ontario
Buffalo, N.Y. 14240-1867	L2A 5X3

YES! Please send me 2 free Harlequin Superromance® novels and my free surprise gift. After receiving them, if I don't wish to receive anymore, I can return the shipping statement marked cancel. If I don't cancel, I will receive 6 brand-new novels every month, before they're available in stores. In the U.S.A., bill me at the bargain price of $4.47 plus 25¢ shipping and handling per book and applicable sales tax, if any*. In Canada, bill me at the bargain price of $4.99 plus 25¢ shipping and handling per book and applicable taxes**. That's the complete price, and a savings of at least 10% off the cover prices—what a great deal! I understand that accepting the 2 free books and gift places me under no obligation ever to buy any books. I can always return a shipment and cancel at any time. Even if I never buy another book from Harlequin, the 2 free books and gift are mine to keep forever.

135 HDN DNT3
336 HDN DNT4

Name	(PLEASE PRINT)	
Address	Apt.#	
City	State/Prov.	Zip/Postal Code

* Terms and prices subject to change without notice. Sales tax applicable in N.Y.
** Canadian residents will be charged applicable provincial taxes and GST.
All orders subject to approval. Offer limited to one per household and not valid to current Harlequin Superromance® subscribers.
® is a registered trademark of Harlequin Enterprises Limited.

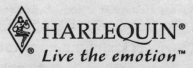

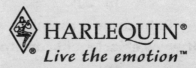

Special thanks and acknowledgment are given
to Stella Bagwell for her contribution to
the MONTANA MAVERICKS:
STRIKING IT RICH miniseries.

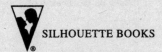 SILHOUETTE BOOKS

ISBN-13: 978-0-373-24843-8
ISBN-10:   0-373-24843-1

PAGING DR. RIGHT

STELLA
BAGWELL

PAGING DR. RIGHT

Silhouette®

SPECIAL **EDITION**®

Published by Silhouette Books

America's Publisher of Contemporary Romance